J. Greenbag Croke

Lyrics of the Law
A Recital of Songs and Verses Pertinent to the Law and the Legal...

ISBN/EAN: 9783744778008

Printed in Europe, USA, Canada, Australia, Japan

Cover: Foto ©Andreas Hilbeck / pixelio.de

More available books at **www.hansebooks.com**

J. Greenbag Croke

Lyrics of the Law

A Recital of Songs and Verses Pertinent to the Law and the Legal...

LYRICS
OF THE LAW.

A RECITAL OF SONGS AND VERSES PERTINENT TO THE
LAW AND THE LEGAL PROFESSION, SELECTED
FROM VARIOUS SOURCES,

–BY–

J. GREENBAG CROKE.

"Come you of the law who can talk if you please,
Till the man in the moon will allow it's a cheese;
And leave the old lady who never tells lies
To sleep with her handkerchief over her eyes."

SAN FRANCISCO:
SUMNER WHITNEY & CO.,
1884.

Mr. Croke, desiring to share with a larger audience the verses read or sung from time to time with little groups of friends, now offers this

RECITAL.

He presents a novel theme, THE LAW, and a programme diversified with song, recitative, chant, and chorus.

The lines are by many hands, the list of contributors forming a galaxy of names renowned in their profession, though unsuspected of lyric powers, such as Sir William Blackstone, John William Smith, Lord Neaves, George Outram, Mr. Justice Story, Judges Joel Parker and R. M. Charlton, *Mr. Punch*, and a host of others.[1]

The music is varied, with airs old as "Malbrook," familiar as "Home Sweet Home," quaint as "Peggie is Over ye Sea," and jolly as "Co-ca-che-lunk."

His recital will not prove an idle amusement, but a moral and instructive recreation, teaching many things touching the law otherwise to be learned only by tedious, sorrowful, and it may be ruinous experience.

Assured of success,[2] he is pleased to announce a second series of more dramatic readings, which will be given at an early day.[3] With this announcement as the preliminary wave of his baton that beribboned emblem of harmonious power is now upheld, for one brief moment motionless, silently soliciting the attention of all.

Signed the 10th day of January, 1834.

J. GREENBAG CROKE.

---

1 Among the names noted in literature here represented are William Cowper, Thomas Moore, Dr. Franklin, John Gibson Lockhart, Dr. Oliver Wendell Holmes, John G. Saxe, Tom Taylor, W. S. Gilbert, and T. H. E. Printer.

2 Always heralded in the play-bills printed before the show.

3 Entitled "Poems of the Law," San Francisco, 1884.

THE PROGRAMME.

Programme.

THE LAW.

THE PROFESSION.

THE PRACTICE.

THE REPORTS.

LYRICS OF THE LAW.

A LAWYER'S FAREWELL TO HIS MUSE.

As by some tyrant's stern command
A wretch forsakes his native land,
In foreign climes condemned to roam,
An endless exile from his home;
Pensive he treads the destined way,
And dreads to go, nor dares to stay;
Till on some neighboring mountain's brow
He stops, and turns his eye below;
There, melting at the well-known view,
Drops a last tear and bids adieu:
So I, thus doom'd from thee to part,
Gay queen of Fancy and of Art,
Reluctant move, with doubtful mind,
Oft stop, and often look behind.

Companion of my tender age,
Serenely gay, and sweetly sage,
How blithesome were we wont to rove
By verdant hill or shady grove,

Where fervent bees, with humming voice,
Around the honey'd oak rejoice,
And aged elms, with awful bend,
In long cathedral walks extend!
Lulled by the lapse of gliding floods,
Cheer'd by the warbling of the woods,
How blest my days, my thoughts how free,
In sweet society with thee!
Then all was joyous, all was young,
And years unheeded roll'd along:
But now the pleasing dream is o'er,
These scenes must charm me now no more.
Lost to the field, and torn from you—
Farewell!—a long, a last adieu.

The wrangling courts and stubborn Law
To smoke, and crowds and cities draw;
There selfish Faction rules the day,
And Pride and Avarice throng the way;
Diseases taint the murky air,
And midnight conflagrations glare;
Loose Revelry and Riot bold
In frighted street their orgies hold;
Or when in silence all is drown'd,
Fell Murder walks her lonely round;
No room for Peace, no room for you—
Adieu, celestial Nymph, adieu!

Shakespeare no more, thy sylvan son,
Nor all the art of Addison,
Pope's heaven-strung lyre, nor Waller's ease,
Nor Milton's mighty self must please;
Instead of these, a formal band
In furs and coifs around me stand,
With sounds uncouth and accents dry,
That grate the soul of harmony.
Each pedant sage unlocks his store
Of mystic, dark, discordant lore,
And points with tott'ring hand the ways
That lead me to the thorny maze.

There, in a winding, close retreat,
Is Justice doom'd to fix her seat;
There, fenc'd by bulwarks of the *Law*,
She keeps the wondering world in awe;
And there, from vulgar sight retired,
Like eastern queens, is much admired.

O, let me pierce the secret shade,
Where dwells the venerable maid!
There humbly mark, with reverent awe,
The guardian of Britannia's Law;
Unfold with joy her sacred page
(The united boast of many an age,

Where mix'd, yet uniform, appears
The wisdom of a thousand years).
In that pure spring the bottom view,
Clear, deep, and regularly true,
And other doctrines thence imbibe,
Than lurk within the sordid scribe;
Observe how parts with parts unite
In one harmonious rule of right;
See countless wheels distinctly tend
By various laws to one great end;
While mighty Alfred's piercing soul
Pervades and regulates the whole.

Then welcome business, welcome strife,
Welcome the cares, the thorns of life,
The visage wan, the pore-blind sight,
The toil by day, the lamp by night,
The tedious forms, the solemn prate,
The pert dispute, the dull debate,
The drowsy bench, the babbling hall—
For thee, fair Justice, welcome all!

Thus, though my noon of life be past,
Yet let my setting sun at last
Find out the still, the rural cell,
Where sage Retirement loves to dwell!

There let me taste the home-felt bliss
Of innocence and inward peace ;
Untainted by the guilty bribe ;
Uncurs'd amid the harpy tribe ;
No orphan's cry to wound my ear;
My honor and my conscience clear:
Thus may I calmly meet my end,
Thus to the grave in peace descend.

LAWYER'S PRAYER.

ORDAIN'D to tread the thorny ground,
Where very few, I fear, are sound;
Mine be the conscience void of blame,
The upright heart, the spotless name,
The tribute of the widow's prayer,
The righted orphan's grateful tear!
To Virtue and her friends a friend,
Still may my voice the weak defend!
Ne'er may my prostituted tongue
Protect the oppressor in his wrong;
Nor wrest the spirit of the laws,
To sanctify the villain's cause!
Let others, with unsparing hand,
Scatter their poison through the land,
Enflame dissension, kindle strife,
And strew with ills the path of life;
On such her gifts let Fortune shower,
Add wealth to wealth and power to power:
On me, may favoring Heaven bestow
That peace which good men only know.
The joy of joys by few possess'd,
The eternal sunshine of the breast!

Power, fame, and riches I resign—
The praise of honesty be mine;
That friends may weep, the worthy sigh,
And poor men bless me when I die!

A FLIGHT OF FANCY.

At the bar of Judge Conscience. stood Reason
    arraign'd,
The jury impanell'd, the prisoner chain'd.
The judge was facetious, at times, though severe,
Now waking a smile, and now drawing a tear;
An old-fashion'd, fidg'ty, queer-looking wight,
With a clerical air, and an eye quick as light.

"Here, Reason, you vagabond! look in my face;.
I'm told you're becoming an idle scapegrace.
They say that young Fancy, that airy coquette,
Has dared to fling round you her luminous net;
That she ran away with you, in spite of yourself,
For pure love of frolic—the mischievous elf.

"The scandal is whispered by friends and by foes,
And darkly they hint too, that when they propose
Any question to *your* ear, so lightly you're led,
At once to gay Fancy you turn your wild head;
And *she* leads you off in some dangerous dance,
As wild as the polka that gallop'd from France.

"Now up to the stars with you, laughing, she
    springs,
With a whirl and a whisk of her changeable wings;

Now dips in some fountain her sun-painted plume,
That gleams thro' the spray like a rainbow in
     bloom;
Now floats in a cloud, while her tresses of light
Shine through the frail boat and illumine its flight;
Now glides through the woodland to gather its
     flowers;
Now darts like a flash to the sea's coral bowers;
In short—cuts such capers, that with her I ween
It's a wonder you are not ashamed to be seen!

"Then she talks such a language! melodious enough,
To be sure—but a strange sort of outlandish stuff!
I'm told that it licenses many a whopper,
And when once she commences no frowning can
     stop her;
Since it's new—I've no doubt it is very improper!
They say that she cares not for order or law;
That of you—you great dunce!—she but makes a
     cat's-paw.
I've no sort of objection to fun in its season,
But it's plain that this Fancy is *fooling* you,
     Reason!"

Just then into court flew a strange little sprite,
With wings of all colors and ringlets of light!

She frolick'd round Reason—till Reason grew wild,
Defying the court and caressing the child.
The judge and the jury, the clerk and recorder,
In vain call'd this exquisite creature to order:—
"Unheard of intrusion!"—They bustled about,
To seize her, but, wild with delight at the rout,
She flew from their touch like a bird from a spray,
And went waltzing and whirling and singing away!

Now up to the ceiling, now down to the floor!
Were never such antics in court-house before!
But a lawyer, well versed in the tricks of his trade,
A trap for the gay little innocent laid:
He held up a *mirror*, and Fancy was caught
By her image within it, so lovely, she thought.
What could the fair creature be? Bending its eyes
On her own with so wistful a look of surprise!
She flew to embrace it. The lawyer was ready!
He closed round the sprite a grasp cool and steady,
And she sigh'd, while he tied her two luminous
  wings,
"Ah! Fancy and Falsehood are different things!"

The witnesses—maidens of uncertain age,
With a critic, a publisher, a lawyer and sage—
All scandalized greatly at what they had heard
Of this poor little Fancy, (who flew like a bird!)

Were call'd to the stand and their evidence gave :
The judge charged the jury, with countenance
    grave.
Their verdict was "guilty," and Reason look'd
    down,
As his honor exhorted her thus, with a frown :—

" This Fancy, this vagrant, for life shall be chain'd
In your own little cell, where *you* should have
    remain'd ;
And you, for *your* punishment, jailer shall be :
Don't let your accomplice come coaxing to me !
I'll none of her nonsense—the little wild witch !
Nor her bribes—although rumor does say she is
    rich.

" I've heard that all treasures and luxuries rare
Gather round at her bidding, from earth, sea, and
    air ;
And some go so far as to hint that the powers
Of darkness attend her more sorrowful hours.
But go !"—and Judge Conscience, who never was
    bought,
Just bow'd the pale prisoner out of the court.

'Tis said that poor Reason next morning was found
At the door of her cell fast asleep on the ground,

And nothing within, but one plume rich and rare,
Just to show that young Fancy's wing once had
    been there.
She had dropped it, no doubt, while she strove to
    get through
The hole in the lock, which she could not undo.

TO A SPARROW

ALIGHTING BEFORE THE JUDGES' CHAMBERS IN SER-
GEANTS' INN, FLEET STREET. WRITTEN IN HALF
AN HOUR, WHILE ATTENDING A SUMMONS.

ART thou solicitor for all thy tribe,
    That thus I now behold thee?—one that comes
Down amid bail-above, an under scribe,
    To sue for crumbs?—
Away! 'tis vain to ogle round the square,—
    I fear thou hast no head,
    To think to get thy bread
Where lawyers are!

Say, hast thou pulled some sparrow o'er the coals,
    And flitted here a summons to indite?
    I only hope no cursed judicial kite
Has struck thee off the rolls!
I scarce should dream thee of the law; and yet
    Thine eye is keen and quick enough; and still
Thou bear'st thyself with perk and tiny fret:
    But then how desperately short thy *bill!*
How quickly might'st thou be of that bereft!
A sixth "taxed off," how little would be left!

Art thou on summons come or order bent?
Tell me, for I am sick at heart to know.
Say, in the sky is there "distress for rent,"
That thou hast flitted to the courts below?
If thou *wouldst* haul some sparrow o'er the coals,
And *wouldst* his spirit hamper and perplex—
Go to John Body—he's available—
Sign, swear, and get a bill of Middlesex,
Returnable (mind, bailable!)
On Wednesday after th' morrow of All Souls.

Or dost thou come a sufferer? I see—
I see thee " cast thy *bail*-ful eyes around ";
O, call James White, and he will set thee free.
He and John Baines will speedily be bound,
In double the sum,
That thou wilt come,
And meet the plaintiff Bird on legal ground.

But stand—O, stand aside!—for look,
Judge Best, on no fantastic toe,
Through dingy arch—by dirty nook—
Across the yard into his room doth go;—
And wisely there doth read
Summons for time to plead,
And frame
Order for same.

Thou twittering, legal, foolish, feather'd thing,
    A tiny boy, with salt for *latitat*,
Is sneaking, bailiff-like, to touch thy wing;—
    Canst thou not see the trick he would be at?
Away, away! and let him not prevail.
    I do rejoice thou'rt off, and yet I groan
    To read in that boy's silly fate my own;
    I am at fault,
    For from my *attic* though I brought my *salt*,
I've failed to put a little on thy *tale*.

    3

ON THE APPROACH OF SPRING.

LINES WRITTEN IN A LAWYER'S OFFICE.

WHEREAS, on certain boughs and sprays,
  Now divers birds are heard to sing,
And sundry flowers their heads upraise—
  Hail to the coming on of Spring.

The songs of those said birds arouse
  The memory of our youthful hours,
As green as those said sprays and boughs,
  As fresh and sweet as those said flowers.

The birds aforesaid—happy pairs!—
  Love 'midst the aforesaid boughs enshrines,
In freehold nests, themselves, their heirs,
  Administrators, and assigns.

O, busiest term of Cupid's court!
  Where tender plaintiffs actions bring;
Season of frolic and of sport,
  Hail, as aforesaid, coming Spring!

SWEET AUTUMN DAYS.

Sweet autumn days, sweet autumn days,
   When, harvest o'er, the reaper slumbers,
How gratefully I hymn your praise,
   In modest but melodious numbers.
But if I'm ask'd why 'tis I make
   Autumn the theme of inspiration,
I'll tell the truth, and no mistake—
   With autumn comes the long vacation.
Of falsehoods I'll not shield me with a tissue—
Autumn I love—because *no writs then issue.*

Others may hail the joys of spring,
   When birds and buds alike are growing;
Some the summer days may sing,
   When sowing, mowing, on are going.
Old winter, with his hoary locks,
   His frosty face and visage murky,
May suit some very jolly cocks,
   Who like roast beef, mince pie, and turkey:
But give me autumn—yes, I'm autumn's child—
For then—*no declarations can be filed.*

PASTORAL FOR THE LONG VACATION.

See Sergeant Tityrus—in rural case,
Forgetting all the cares of Common Pleas,
Taking beneath some shady beech his station,
To sip the honey of the long vacation.
Ye nymphs, beware should Tityrus seek your grove,
For his "attachment" is no name for love.
The gentle lamblings cluster idly round,
Lured by his legal pipe's too dulcet sound.
Ah! little do ye think, ye simple sheep,
(Or at a greater distance ye would keep,)
That he whose plaintive strains ye flock to hear,
Knows not a greater pleasure than to shear.
Viewing your curling fleece, it o'er him flits,
The hide beneath is meant to furnish writs;
While all the woolly treasures on your back
He hopes one day may stuff for him the sack.

TRILLS FOR TERM-TIME.

How sweet 'tis to stroll by the streams of Demurrer,
    Where Detinue sighs to the evening breeze;
Where groves of Mandamus are mellowed in color,
    And high soar the Costs in Exchequer of Pleas.

'Tis there that the sisters Assumpsit and Trover
    Disport with the Mortgages sitting in banc,
While around the fierce Chattels and Cognizance
        hover,
    And Rejoinders gnash rage as their fetters they
        clank.

Dark Venue broods there, 'mid the bleak Certiorari,
    The coo of the distant Avowry is heard;
But the sprightly Malfeazance trips light as a fairy,
    With the mild Surrebutter and Judgment De-
        ferred.

O, 'tis there I would muse, and I'd dream of Assizes
    And feast on ripe Codicil and Assignee;
Or, soothed by the strain of the dulcet Demises,
    I'd quaff foaming goblets of Felo-de-se.

A RESPONSE.

His Honor's father yet remains
   His proud paternal posture firm in;
But, while his right he still maintains
To wield the household rod and reins,
   He bows before the filial ermine.

What curious tales has life in store,
   With all its must-bes and its may-bes!
The sage of eighty years and more
Once crept a nursling on the floor—
   Kings, conquerors, judges, all were babies.

The fearless soldier who has faced
   The serried bayonets' gleam appalling,
For nothing save a pin misplaced
The peaceful nursery has disgraced
   With hours of unheroic bawling.

The mighty monarch, whose renown
   Fills up the stately page historic,
Has howled to waken half the town,
And finished off by gulping down
   His castor oil or paregoric.

The justice, who in gown and cap
   Condemns a wretch to strangulation,
Has scratched his nurse and spilled his pap,
And sprawled across his mother's lap
   For wholesome laws' administration.

Ah! life has many a reef to shun
   Before in port we drop our anchor;
But when its course is nobly run,
Look aft! for there the work was done:
   Life owes its headway to the spanker.

Yon seat of justice well might awe
   The fairest manhood's half-blown summer;
There Parsons scourged the laggard law,
There reigned and ruled majestic Shaw—
   What ghosts to hail the last new-comer!

One cause of fear I faintly name—
   The dread lest duty's dereliction
Shall give so rarely cause for blame,
Our guileless voters will exclaim,
   "No need of human jurisdiction!"

What keeps the doctors' trade alive?
   Bad air, bad water; more's the pity!

But lawyers walk where doctors drive,
And starve in streets where surgeons thrive,
   Our Boston is so pure a city.

What call for court or judge, indeed,
   When righteousness prevails so through it?
Our virtuous car-conductors need
Only a card whereon they read:
   "Do right; it's naughty not to do it!"

The whirligig of time goes round,
   And changes all things but affection;
One blessed comfort may be found
In heaven's broad statute, which has bound
   Each household to its head's protection.

If e'er aggrieved, attacked, accused,
   A sire may claim a son's devotion
To shield his innocence abused,
As old Anchises freely used
   His offspring's legs for locomotion.

You smile. You did not come to weep,
   Nor I my weakness to be showing;
And these gay stanzas, slight and cheap,
Have served their simple use—to keep
   A father's eyes from overflowing.

NONSUITED.

In Cupid's Court when *suit* is brought
    Attachment must precede it;
For when a final *judgment's* reached,
    The *plaintiff's* sure to need it.

The wee, blind judge is very wroth
    If legal *forms* are slighted ;
But if a *case* is clearly *made*
    His Honor is delighted.

Prolonged *complaints* he ne'er approves,
    Submission never warrants;
Misjoined the *parties* must not be—
    This is his chief abhorrence.

An honest, earnest *plea* is best—
    It brings no vain *demurring ;*
The *issues* then are quickly joined,
    And soon may come *concurring.*

If he may *take* who fears to lose,
    Is still a question mooted;
But who declines *a tender made*
    Must surely be *nonsuited.*

THE SPECIAL PLEADER'S LAMENT.

TO ———.

Say, Mary, canst thou sympathize
 With one whose heart is bleeding,
Compell'd to wake from "love's young dream,"
 And take to special pleading?

For, since I lost my suit to you,
 I care not now a fraction
About these tiresome suits of law,
 These senseless forms of action.

But in my lonely chambers, oft
 When clients leave me leisure,
In musing o'er departed joys,
 I find a mournful pleasure.

How well I know the spot where first
 I saw thy form ethereal!
But ah! in transitory things
 The venue's not material;

And, reading Archbold's Practice now,
 I scarce believe 'tis true,

That I could set my heart upon
  An *arch*, *bold* girl like you.

But then that bright blue eye sent forth
  A most unerring dart,
Which, like a *special capias*, made
  A pris'ner of my heart.

And in the weakness of my soul,
  One fatal, long vacation,
I gave a pledge to prosecute,
  And filed a declaration.

At first, your taking time to plead
  Gave hopes for my felicity;
The doubtful negative you spoke,
  Seem'd bad for its duplicity.

And then that blush so clearly seem'd
  To pardon my transgression;
I thought I was about to snap
  A judgment by confession.

But soon I learned (most fatal truth!)
  How rashly I had counted:
For, *non assumpsit* was the plea
  To which it all amounted.

Deceitful maid! another swain
  Was then beloved by thee;
The *preference* you gave to him
  Was *fraudulent* to me.

[But then, alas! the Barons held
  The transfer of this treasure
Could not by me be set aside,
  Being made when *under pressure.*]

Ah! when we love (so Shakspeare says)
  Bad luck is sure to have us;
The course of true love never ran
  Without some *special traverse.*

Say, what *inducement* could you have
  To act so base a part?
Without this that you smiled on me,
  I ne'er had lost my heart.

My rival I was doom'd to see
  A husband's rights assert;
And now 'tis wrong to think of you,
  For you're a *feme covert.*

When last I saw your son and heir,
  'Twas wormwood for a lover;

But then the plea of infancy
   My heart could not get over.

I kiss'd the little brat, and said,
   "Much happiness I wish you,"
But oh! I felt he was to me
   An *immaterial issue!*

Mary, adieu! I'll mourn no more,
   Nor pen pathetic ditties;
My pleading was of no avail,
   And so I'll stick to Chitty's.

4

LAW-LOVE.

THE burning of a man's abode
Is punished by the Penal Code,
   With loss of life or lands;
Then surely that offense, more dire,
Of setting all his heart on fire,
   Fit penalty demands.

Dear, guilty girl—thou guilty dear—
The plaintiff cites you to appear
   In presence of the parson
(He grants that you may fix the day),
To answer in the usual way
   This last aforesaid Arson.

Do not your tender guilt deny,
But own it, darling, with a sigh;
   I long for judgment by confession:
Do not affect the law's delay,
And force me still to plead and pray;
   Concede my right and yield possession.

LINES TO BESSY.

My heart is like a title-deed,
  Or abstract of the same;
Wherein, my Bessy, thou may'st read
  Thine own long-cherish'd name.

Against thee I my suit have brought,
  I am thy plaintiff lover,
And for the heart that thou hast caught,
  An action lies—of trover.

Alas! upon me every day
  The heaviest costs you levy;
O give me back my heart—but nay!
  I feel I can't replevy.

I'll love thee with my latest breath,
  Alas! I cannot *you* shun,
Till the hard grasp of Sheriff death
  Takes me in execution.

Say, Bessy dearest, if you will
  Accept me as a lover?
Must true affection file a bill
  The secret to discover?

Is it my income's small amount
That leads to hesitation?
Refer the question of account
To Cupid's arbitration.

LAW AT OUR BOARDING-HOUSE.

As fresh as a pink, on the other side
    Of the boarding-house table she sits, and sips
Her tea; while I envy the china cup
    That kisses her rosy lips.

She's a school-girl still in her teens; her hair
    She wears in a plait; we are *vis-à-vis;*
And I am a briefless barrister ;—
    Yet she sometimes smiles at me.

My law professor would scowl, no doubt,
    Could he know what havoc those eyes have
        wrought
With the doctrines of law he first instilled—
    What lessons those lips have taught.

" Attachment can never come before
    A declaration," he used to say ;
But this little girl at our boarding-house
    Doesn't put the thing that way.

" The clerk will issue a rule to plead—
    And pleadings always with rules must chime ";
No need for " a rule to plead " with her—
    And her rule-days are—all the time !

The old law maxim, the text-books teach,
　And the judges regard : " *Qui facit per*
Alium, facit per se," is held
　In ineffable scorn by her.

In her person exist together at once
　Defendant and judge and jury and clerk ;
So that one would imagine to win a cause
　In this court were an up-hill work.

Yet whenever I sit at the table there,
　I fancy a table where only two
Are company—till I say to myself :
　" Though you lose the case, why sue !

" E'en though she demur at first—who knows ?—
　For the rest of your joint lives made one life,
You may learn together the lesson taught
　In respect to Husband and Wife."

Still I dally in doubt ; though in other things
　I flatter myself I am resolute :
For a bankrupt heart will be the result,
　If I'm taxed with costs in this suit.

THE LAWYER'S VALENTINE.

I'm notified, fair neighbor mine,
   By one of our profession,
That this—the Term of Valentine—
   Is Cupid's Special Session.

Permit me, therefore, to report
   Myself, on this occasion,
Quite ready to proceed to Court,
   And File my Declaration.

I've an Attachment for you, too;
   A legal and a strong one;
O, yield unto the Process, do;
   Nor let it be a long one!

No scowling bailiff lurks behind;
   He'd be a precious noddy,
Who, failing to Arrest the mind,
   Should go and Take the Body!

For though a form like yours might throw
   A sculptor in distraction;
I couldn't serve a Capias—no,
   I'd scorn so base an Action!

O, do not tell me of your youth,
  And turn away demurely;
For though you're very young, in truth,
  You're not an Infant surely!

The Case is everything to me;
  My heart is love's own tissue;
Don't plead a Dilatory Plea;
  Let's have the General Issue!

Or, since you've really no Defense,
  Why not, this present Session,
Omitting all absurd pretense,
  Give judgment by Confession?

So shall you be my lawful wife;
  And I—your faithful lover—
Be Tenant of your heart for Life,
  With no Remainder over!

THE LAWYER'S SUIT.

Air—"For the Lack of Gold."

O why, lady, why, when I come to your side,
Repulse your poor suitor with such haughty pride?
That you'll never wed with a Lawyer you swear—
But why so averse to a Lawyer, my dear?

Can it be, that because I have thought and have
    read,
Till my heart to the world and its pleasures is dead?
Pshaw! my heart may be hard, but then it is clear
Your triumph's the greater to melt it, my dear!

Can it be that because my eyes have grown dim,
And my color is wan, and my body is slim?
Pshaw! the husk of the almond as rough does ap-
    pear—
But what do you think of the kernel, my dear?

Would you wed with a Fop full of apish grimace,
Whose antics would call all the blood to your face?
Take me, from confusion you're sure to be clear,
For a Lawyer's ne'er troubled with blushes, my
    dear!

Would you wed with a Merchant, who'd curse and
    who'd bann
'Cause he's plagued by his conscience for cheating
    a man?
Take me, and be sure that my conscience is clear,
For a Lawyer's ne'er troubled with conscience, my
    dear!

Would you wed with a Soldier with brains made
    of fuel,
Who, defending his honor, is killed in a duel?
Take me, and such danger you've no need to fear,
For my honor is not worth defending, my dear!

Come, wed with a Lawyer! you needn't fear strife,
For since I have borne with the courts all my life,
That the Devil can't ruffle my temper, I'll swear—
And I hardly think you could do't either, my dear!

TO ——, THE LAWYER.

LEND me your ears, thou man of law,
While I my declaration draw—
   Your heart in fee surrender;
As plaintiff I my suit prefer,
'Twould be uncivil to demur,
   Then let your plea be—tender.

On certain promises I sue,
Given at sundry times by you,
   O, does not it unnerve thee!
When urged by passion's boldest fits,
I issue one of Cupid's writs,
   And with it boldly serve thee!

Appear in person, I beseech,
Nor resignation idly teach
   To one already lost, sir;
Proceedings I will only stay
Upon condition that you pay
   At once the debt and costs, sir.

Then take my heart, be not a brute,
But ask a rule—just to compute
   The misery of its state, man;

Some people's minds are wildly thrown
At sixes and at sev'ns I own;
   Mine's all at six and eight, man.

List to the evidence that I
Of my affection here supply,
   Examine well my heart, now;
It beats with such tremendous force,
That its mere motion ("quite" of course)
   Is like a jolting cart, now.

My judgment by default is gone,
And I, alas! go raving on,
   For fear you should forsake me;
There's no defense—don't be a brute,
I give you a rule absolute.
   In execution take me.

By act of Parliament alone,
But by no action of your own,
   A gentleman they call you;
What's that to me? though slander's rife,
I'm still prepared to be your wife,
   Although disgrace befall you.

Your dirty pettifogging tricks
May on you others' hatred fix,
   I heed not their reflections ;
My passion now defies control,
I cannot strike you off the roll
   Of my sincere affections.

   5

A Moan from the San Francisco Bar,

On losing an Esteemed Lady Member.

Alas! that Mary should unfaithful be
To cheerful Law and gladsome Equity;
That the bright legal prom'se erst she made
Thus quickly from her woman's mind should fade;
And all the glories of forensic strife
Should mist-like banish from her dream of life.
No more to Themis doth her homage lie,
Her Kent and Blackstone laid forever by,
Her brain no more perplexed with Law's conjectures,
Her eloquence confined to curtain-lectures.

'Mid what grand projects did her day-dreams pass!
"No quibbling fright she'd be! No Sally Brass!
But something nobly feminine, to force ne
To admiration, — like Antonio's Portia."
But mark! Subdued and meek, she standeth now,
With crimsoned cheek, — confusion on her brow, —
Gone all her legal tact and shrewd acumen, —
Her nature all confessed, — a very woman.

Her downfall happened in this curious wise:
Astræa wears a bandage o'er her eyes;
But there's another deity that's blinded, —
An infant scapegrace, sly and evil-minded, —
Who one day prowled about in search of sport,
And clambered on the bench and opened court;
There stood our Mary, fumbling o'er her papers,
Unwitting the *de facto* judge's capers.

Quoth he, "This maid would make the rash attempt
To oust my jurisdiction! Rank contempt!"
And while she trembling tried her pleading art,
The arch-rogue clapped in custody her heart;
And so while deftly weaving legal snares,
In Cupid's toils, lo! Mary falls unwares.

A canny Scot, as full of man's deceit
As ever new-laid egg was full of meat,
Was named as bailiff, on his firm assurance
He'd keep the recreant for aye in durance;
But why waste tropes in plaining our mishap?
Our Mary's gone off with an artist chap!
The crafty man of landscapes, tuips, and brushes
Cepit our Mary, spite demurring blushes;
And with a cool defiance flung *in curiam,*
Comes to dly and defends *vim et injuriam.*

Mary, good-bye, we must forgive the *tort;*
At least, you've won your case in Cupid's Court;
Your *status* henceforth, — may't prove no *servitium,*
And no beginning, but a *finis litium;*
And may you ne'er encounter that fell woe
Of woman's life, — *divorce a vinculo;*
Or find, in time, a trusting wife's *deliciæ*
Turning, midst married storms, to sour *sævitiæ;*
And be the latest Mem. upon your docket,
"A baby's cradle, — how to stock and rock it."

PROFESSIONAL LOVE SONG.

SPINSTER of the Saxon beauty,
    At the Grainthrope Manor mill,
Of this heart you've had possession
    Since I made my uncle's will:
Yours the image all-engrossing,
    When I try to read Reports,
You, my Amy, am I drawing,
    Even in the Chancery Courts.

Ah! that brow as smooth as—vellum—
    Ah! those lips vermilion red—
Kisses wherewith I have sealed them
    No one ever witnesséd:
I would sue the man who ventured
    To deny you dressed with taste,
I would tax his costs who hinted
    An "impeachment" of your waist.

Soon the long vacation's coming,
    Soon the weary term will end;
No more writs and affidavits,
    No more actions to defend:
I shall take the first conveyance—
    Train at 5 P. M.—express—

I shall count the sluggish moments—
    Forty minutes, more or less.

Meet me, cousin, at the station
    With the trap that's duty free,
It can take my rods and gun-case,
    We will walk, *prochein*, Amy,
Past the glebe and old inclosure,
    Past the deeply mortgaged inn,
On to where the freeholds finish
    And the copyholds begin.

There I'll make my declaration,
    There I'll pause and plead my suit;
Do not let it be "in error,"
    Do not be of malice mute;
But "surrender" to your cousin
    In the customary way,
And become the donee, dearest,
    Of an opal *negligée.*

I've a messuage—recent purchase—
    Sixty-eight in Mortmayne Row,
Title good, and unencumbered,
    Gas and water laid below;
Come and share it, undisputed
    Owner of this heart, in fee,

Come and be my junior partner,
 And my better moiety:
J. P. Wilde shall never part us,
 And in time we both may see
Girls, fair copies of their mother;
 Boys, the counterpart of me.

THE LAWYER'S STRATAGEM.

A GAY young spark, who long had sighed
To take an heiress for his bride,
Though not in vain he had essayed
To win the favor of the maid,
Yet fearing, from his humble station,
To meet her father's cold negation,
Made up his mind, without delay,
To take the girl and run away!
A pretty plan—what could be finer?—
But as the maid was yet a minor,
There still remained this slight obstruction:
He might be punished for " abduction!"
Accordingly, he thought it wise
To see the squire and take advice—
A cunning knave who loved a trick
As well as fees, and skilled to pick,
As lawyers can, some latent flaw
To help a client cheat the law.
Before him straight the case was laid,
Who, when the proper fee was paid,
Conceived at once a happy plan,
And thus the counsellorbegan:
"Young man, no doubt your wisest course
Is this: to-night, you get a horse,

And let your lady-love get on;
As soon as ever that is done,
 You get on too—but, hark ye! mind
She rides before; *you* ride *behind;*
And thus, you see, you make it true,
The lady runs away with you!"
That very night he got the horse,
And put the lawyer's plan in force;
Who found next day—no laughing matter—
The truant lady was his daughter.

MORAL.

When lawyers counsel craft and guile,
It may, sometimes, be worth the while,
If they'd avoid the deepest shames,
To ascertain the parties' names.

LOVE AND LAW.

A LEGEND OF BOSTON.

JACK NEWMAN was in love; a common case
   With boys just verging upon manhood's prime,
When every damsel with a pretty face
   Seems some bright creature from a purer clime,
Sent by the gods to bless a country town—
A pink-cheeked angel in a muslin gown.

Jack was in love; and also much in doubt
   (As thoughtful lovers oft have been before)
If it were better to be in or out.
   Such pain alloyed his bliss.   On reason's score,
Perhaps 'tis equally a sin to get
Too deep in love, in liquor, or in debt.

The lady of his love, Miss Mary Blank
   (I call her so to hide her real name),
Was fair and twenty, and in social rank—
   That is, in riches—much above her flame;
The daughter of a person who had tin
Alrea'y won; while Jack had his to win.

Her father was a lawyer; rather rusty
   In legal lore, but one who well had striven

In former days to swell his "*res augustæ*"
    To broad possessions; and, in short, had thriven
Bravely in his vocation; though, the fact is,
    More by his "practices" ('twas said) than practice!

A famous name was Blank for sound advice
    In doubtful cases; for example, where
The point in question is extremely nice,
    And turns upon the section of a hair;
Or where—which seems a very common pother—
Justice looks one way, and the Law another.

Great was his skill to make or mar a plot;
    To prop, at need, a rotten reputation,
Or undermine a good one; he had got
    By heart the subtle science of evasion,
And knew the useful art to pick a flaw
Through which a rascal might escape the law.

Jack was his pupil; and 'tis rather queer
    So shrewd a counsellor did not discover,
With all his cunning both of eye and ear,
    That this same pupil was his daughter's lover;
And, what would much have shocked his legal tutor,
Was even now the girl's accepted suitor!

Fearing a *non-suit*, if the lawyer knew
    The case too soon, Jack kept it to himself;

And, stranger still, the lady kept it too ;
   For well he knew the father's pride of pelf,
Should e'en a bare suspicion cross his mind,
Would soon abate the action they designed.

For Jack was impecunious; and Blank
   Had small regard for people who were poor;
Riches to him were beauty, grace, and rank:
   In short, the man was one of many more
Who worship money-bags and those who own 'em,
And think a handsome sum the *summum bonum.*

I'm fond of civil words, and do not wish
   To be satirical ; but none despise
The poor so truly as the *nouveaux riche ;*
   And here, no doubt, the real reason lies,
That being over-proud of what they are,
They're naturally ashamed of what they were.

Certain to meet the father's cold negation,
   Jack dare not ask him for his daughter's hand.
What should he do ? 'Twas surely an occasion
   For all the wit a lover might command ;
At last he chose (it seemed his only hope)
That final card of Cupid—to elope!

A pretty plan to please a penny-a-liner;
   But far less pleasant for the leading factor.

Should the fair maiden chance to be a *minor*
   (Whom the law reckons an unwilling actor);
And here Jack found a rather sad obstruction—
He might be caught and punished for abduction.

What could he do? Well—here is what he did:
   As a "moot-case" to Lawyer Blank he told
The whole affair, save that the names were hid.
   I can't help thinking it was rather bold,
But Love is partial to heroic schemes,
And often proves much wiser than he seems.

"The thing is safe enough, with proper care,"
   Observed the lawyer, smiling. "Here's your
     course:
Just let the lady manage the affair
   Throughout; *Videlicet,* she gets the horse,
And mounts him, unassisted, *first;* but mind,
The woman sits before, and you, behind!

"Then who is the abductor?—Just suppose
   A court and jury looking at the case;
What ground of action do the facts disclose?
   They find a horse—two riders—and a race—
And you 'Not guilty'; for 'tis clearly true
The dashing damsel ran away with you!"

    *   *   *   *   *   *

These social sins are often rather grave;
   I give such deeds no countenance of mine.
Nor can I say the father e'er forgave;
   But that was surely a propitious " sign,"
On which (in after years) the words I saw
Were, " BLANK AND NEWMAN, COUNSELLORS AT
    LAW ! "

6

IN WOMAN'S PRAISE.

Strike, O Legal Muse, thy lyre,
   In lovely woman's praise,
Who sheds a lustre 'round our lives
   And brightens all our days!

She's been the glory of the world,
   E'er since said world began;
And to the contrary runneth not
   The memory of man.

Whereas, her face is beautiful
   (To wit: her eyes of light,
And divers rosy, pouting lips,
   And sundry cheeks so bright;

Likewise her fair and noble brow,
   Her lovely smile and dimple)—
She holds possession of our souls
   In absolute fee-simple.

Her title to our hearts was fixed,
   By Heaven's adjudication,
And never can our love for her
   Expire by limitation.

In all the divers walks of life
    She sways a queenly sceptre :
There is no one upon the earth
    Who rules the heart, except her.

Under full age, as sweetheart dear
    (Such is our firm conviction),
She rules all those who come to court
    Within her jurisdiction.

She sits as Judge in Love's Moot Court,
    To hear pleas of the soul,
And issue warrants of distress,
    Tho' always by parol.

But when, at last, the lucky one,
    His declaration files,
A fond Attachment is confessed
    With many blushing smiles;

And then with valid notice given,
    The ecclesiastics come,
And join in Special Partnership
    " Two hearts that beat as one."

And all through life, as mother, wife
    (The world will indorse these sentiments),

Our messuages she fills with joy,
    And gladdens all our tenements.

She is an angel on the earth,
    A goddess, warm and true;
Such was she thought at Common Law,
    And in America too.

And now we've tried, as herein shown,
    Her glories to reveal;
And this we are ready to verify:
    Witness our hand and seal.

                JOHN DOE. [SEAL.]

AN OLD SAW.

An upper mill and lower mill
   Fell out about their water;
To war they went—that is, to law—
   Resolved to give no quarter.

A lawyer was by each engaged,
   And hotly they contended;
When fees grew scant, the war they waged
   They judged were better ended.

The heavy costs remaining still
   Were settled without pother:
One lawyer took the upper mill,
   The lower mill the other.

LAW, A COMIC SONG.

Air.—"Malbrook."

Come list to me a minute,
A song I'm going to begin it,
There's something serious in it.
    So pray attention draw,
    'Tis all about the Law,
    So pray attention draw.
Experience I have bought it,
And now to you I've brought it
Will you or not be taught it?
    I sing the charms of Law.
    L-A-W—law,
    Which has met with a deuce of *eclat.*
If you're fond of pure vexation,
And long procrastination,
You're just in a situation
    To enjoy a suit at law.

When your cause is first beginning,
You only think of winning,
Attorneys slyly grinning,
    The while the cash they draw;
    Your cause goes on see-saw,
    As long as your cash they draw;

With brief and consultation,
Bill and replication,
Latin and—botheration,
   While the counsel loudly jaw;
   J–A–W—jaw,
   Is a very great thing in law.
If you're fond, etc.

Snail-like your cause is creeping,
It hinders you from sleeping,
Attorneys only reaping,
   For still your cash they draw;
   D–R–A–W—draw,
   Is the mainspring of the law,
Misery, toil, and trouble,
Make up the hubble, bubble,
Leave you nothing but stubble,
   And make you a man of straw.
   L–A–W—law,
   Divides the wheat from the straw.
If you're fond, etc.

And when your cause is ending,
Your case is no way mending,
Expense each step attending,
   And then they find a flaw.
   Then the judge, like any jack-daw,
   Will lay down what is Law.

In a rotten stick your trust is,　　.
You find the bubble burst is,
And though you don't get justice,
　　You're sure to get plenty of Law.
　　And L-A-W—law,
　　Leaves you not worth a straw.
If you're fond, etc.

So if life is all sugar and honey.
And fortune has always been sunny,
And you want to get rid of your money,
　　I'd advise you to go to law.
　　Like ice in a rapid thaw,
　　Your cash will melt awa';
Comfort 'tis folly to care for,
Life's a lottery—therefore
Without a why or a wherefore,
　　I'd advise you to go to law,
　　And L-A-W—law,
　　Does like a blister draw.
If you're fond, etc.

THE ANNUITY.

Air—"Duncan Davidson."

I GAED to spend a week in Fife—
    An unco week it proved to be—
For there I met a waesome wife
    Lamentin' her viduity.
Her grief brak out sae fierce and fell,
I thought her heart wad burst the shell;
And—I was sae left to mysel'—
    I sell't her an annuity.

The bargain lookit fair eneugh—
    She just was turned o' saxty-three;
I couldna guessed she'd prove sae teugh,
    By human ingenuity.
But years have come and years have gane,
And there she's yet as stieve's a stane—
The limmer's growin' young again,
    Since she got her annuity.

She's crined awa' to bane an' skin,
    But that it seems is naught to me;
She's like to live—although she's in
    The last stage o' tenuity.

She munches wi' her wizened gums,
An' stumps about on legs o' thrums,
But comes—as sure as Christmas comes—
   To ca' for her annuity.

She jokes her joke an' cracks her crack,
   As spunkie as a growin' flea—
An' there she sits upon my back,
   A livin' perpetuity.
She hurkles by her ingle side,
An' toasts an' tans her wrunkled hide—
Lord kens how lang she yet may bide
   To ca' for her annuity!

I read the tables drawn wi' care
   For an insurance company;
Her chance o' life was stated there,
   Wi' perfect perspicuity.
But tables here or tables there,
She's lived ten years beyond her share,
An's like to live a dizzen mair,
   To ca' for her annuity.

I gat the loon that drew the deed—
   We spelled it o'er right carefully;—
In vain he yerked his souple head,
   To find an ambiguity:

It's dated—teste'd—a' complete—
The proper stamp—nae word delete—
And diligence, as on decreet,
  May pass for her annuity.

Last Yule she had a fearfu' hoast—
  I thought a kink might set me free;
I led her out 'mang snaw and frost,
  Wi' constant assiduity.
But Diel ma' care—the blast gaed by,
And missed the auld anatomy;
It just cost me a tooth, forbye
  Discharging her annuity.

I thought that grief might gar her quit—
  Her only son was lost at sea—
But aff her wits behuved to flit,
  An' leave her in fatuity!
She threeps, an' threeps, he's livin' yet,
For a' the tellin' she can get;
But catch the doited runt forget
  To ca' for her annuity.

If there's a sough o' cholera
  Or typhus—wha sae gleg as she?
She buys up baths, an' drugs, an' a',
  In siccan superfluity!

She doesna need—she's fever proof—
The pest gaed o'er her very roof;
She tauld me sae—an' then her loof
   Held out for her annuity.

Ae day she fell—her arm she brak—
   A compound fracture as could be;
Nae Leech the cure wad undertak,
   Whate'er was the gratuity.
It's cured!—She handles't like a flail—
It does as weel in bits as hale;
But I'm a broken man mysel',
   Wi' her and her annuity.

Her broozled flesh and broken banes
   Are weel as flesh an' banes can be.
She beats the taeds that live in stanes,
   An' fatten in vacuity!
They die when they're exposed to air—
They canna thole the atmosphere;
But her!—expose her onywhere—
   She lives for her annuity.

If mortal means could nick her thread,
   Sma' crime it wad appear to me;
Ca't murder, or ca't homicide,
   I'd justify't—an' do it tae.

But how to fell a withered wife
That's carved out o' the tree 'o' life—-
The timmer limmer daurs the knife
    To settle her annuity.

I'd try a shot: but whar's the mark?—
    Her vital parts are hid frae me;
Her backbane wanders through her sark
    In an unkenn'd corkscrewity.
She's palsified—an' shakes her head
Sae fast about, ye scarce can see't;
It's past the power o' steel or lead
    To settle her annuity.

She might be drowned—but go she'll not
    Within a mile o' loch or sea;
Or hanged—if cord could grip a throat
    O' siccan exiguity.
It's fitter far to hang the rope—
It draws out like a telescope;
'Twad tak a dreadfu' length o' drop
    To settle her annuity.

Will puzion do't?—It has been tried;
    But, be't in hash or fricassee,
That's just the dish she can't abide,
    Whatever kind o' *goût* it hae.

It's needless to assail her doubts—
She gangs by instinct, like the brutes;
An' only eats an' drinks what suits
    Hersel' an' her annuity.

The Bible says the age o' man
    Threescore an' ten perchance may be;
She's ninety-four;—let them wha can
    Explain the incongruity.
She should hae lived afore the flood—
She's come o' patriarchal blood—
She's some auld pagan, mummified,
    Alive for her annuity.

She's been embalmed inside and out—
    She's sauted to the last degree—
There's pickle in her very snout
    Sae caper-like an' cruety;
Lot's wife was fresh compared to her;
They've kyanized the useless knir—
She canna decompose—nae mair
    Than her accurs'd annuity.

The water-drap wears out the rock,
    As this eternal jaud wears me;
I could withstand the single shock,
    But no the continuity.

It's pay me here an' pay me there—
An' pay me, pay me, evermair;
I'll gang demented wi' despair—
   I'm *charged* for her annuity!

THE ANNUITANT'S ANSWER.

My certy! but it sets him weel
    Sae vile a tale to tell o' me;
I never could suspect the chiel
    O' sic disingenuity.
I'll no be ninety-four for lang,
My health is far frae being strang,
And he'll mak' profit, richt or wrang,
    Ye'll see, by this annuity.

My friends, ye weel can understand
    This world is fu' o' roguery;
And ane meets folk on ilka hand
    To rug and rive and pu' at ye.
I thought that this same man o' law
Wad save my siller frae them a',
And sae I gave the whilliewha
    The note for the annuity.

He says the bargain lookit fair,
    And sae to him, I'm sure 'twad be;
I got my hundred pounds a year,
    An' he could well allow it, tae.

An' does he think—the deevil's limb—
Although I lookit auld and grim,
I was to die to pleasure him,
   And squash my braw annuity.

The year had scarcely turned its back
   When he was irking to be free—
A fule the thing to undertak',
   And then sae sune to rue it ye.
I've never been at peace sin' syne—
Nae wonder that sae sair I coyne—
It's jist through terror that I tyne
   My life for my annuity.

He's twice had pushion in my kail,
   And sax times in my cup o' tea;
I could unfauld a shocking tale
   O' something in a cruet, tae.
His arms he ance flang round my neck—
I thought it was to show respeck;
He only meant to gie a check,
   Not for, but to, the annuity.

Said ance to me an honest man,
   "Try an insurance company;
Ye'll find it an effective plan
   Protection to secure to you.

Ten pounds a year!—ye weel can spare't!
Be that wi' Peter Frazer wared;
His office syne will be a guard
   For you and your annuity."

I gaed at once an' spak' to Pate
   O' a five hundred policy,
And " Faith!" says he, " ye are nae blate;
   I maist could clamahewit ye,
Wi' that chiel's fingers at the knife,
What chance hae ye o' length o' life?
Sae to the door, ye silly wife,
   Wi' you and your annuity."

The procurator fiscal's now
   The only friend that I can see;
And it's sma' thing that he can do
   To end this sair ankshiwity.
But honest Maurice has agreed
That if the villain does the deed,
He'll swing at Libberton Wyndhead
   For me and my annuity.

A FRAGMENT.

IF ye've been up ayont Dundee,
Ye maun hae heard about the plea
That's raised by Sandy Grant's trustee
   For the mill that belang'd to Sandy.
For Sandy lent the man his mill,
An' the mill that was lent was Sandy's mill,
An' the man got the len' o' Sandy's mill,
   An' the mill it belang'd to Sandy.

A' sense o' sin an' shame is gone,
They're claiming noo a lien on
   The mill that belang'd to Sandy.
But Sandy lent the man his mill,
An' the mill that was lent was Sandy's mill,
An' the man got the len' o' Sandy's mill,
   An' the mill it belang'd to Sandy.

MINIMUM DE MALIS.

CALENUS owed a single pound, which yet
With all my dunning I could never get.
Tired of fair words, whose falsehood I foresaw,
I hied to Aulus, learned in the law.
He heard my story, bade me " Never fear,
There was no doubt—no case could be more clear;
He'd do the needful in the proper place,
And give his best attention to the case."

And this he may have done, for it appears
To have been his business for the last ten years;
Though on his pains ten times ten pounds bestowed
Have not acquired that one Calenus owed.

Now, fearful lest this unproductive strife
Consume at once my fortune and my life,
I take the only course I can pursue,
And shun my debtor and my lawyer too.
I've no more hope from promises or laws,
And heartily renounce both debt and cause;
But if with either rogue I've more to do,
I'll surely choose my debtor of the two;
For though I credit not the lies he tells,
At least he *gives* me what the other *sells*.

LAY OF GASCOIGNE JUSTICE.

CHAUNTED BY COOKE AND COKE, SERGEANTS, AND
PLOWDEN, APPRENTICE, IN THE HALL OF SER-
GEANTS' INN, A. D. 15—.

KING HENRY the Fourth
Was a monarch of worth;
But the eldest son of his loins
Was a profligate lad,
Who kept company bad—
Jack Falstaff, Peto, and Poins.

And while the good king
Caused felons to swing,
And guarded each alley and by-way,
The prince, his son,
Considered it fun
To rob in his governor's highway.

And while Henry the Great,
For the good of the State,
Was depriving himself of his sleep,
His son and fat Jack
Were guzzling burnt sack
At the Boar's Head in Eastcheap.

Where, lo and behold,
To him it was told,
There's a carl on the road from Dover,
Whose pockets infold
As much silver and gold
As would blow us all out twice over.

Then straightway rose the noble prince
And lustily cried he,
Now who will stand on either hand,
And take this purse with me.

Then up rose filching Peto,
Of Newgate blood was he,
I will cry, Stand, on thy right hand,
And take the purse with thee.

And up rose Poins, the footpad,
Of Tyburn race was he,
I will abide by thy left side,
And take this purse with thee.
Then straightway forth to Shooter's Hill
Wended the dauntless three.

Soon as the deed of dole was done,
The neighbors shouted, Fie !

And straight they to the sheriff run,
　　And raise the hue and cry.

Catch me the rogues, the sheriff cried,
　　They're fruit for Tyburn tree;
Now ride and run, now run and ride,
　　For arrant knaves they be.

Heav'n save them, quoth Jack Falstaff,
　　And send them safe to town;
For such a valiant deed has ne'er
　　Been done by lord or lown.

Now swiftly run the constables,
　　With oilskin hats and capes;
They caught the prince—but let him go
　　With many bows and scrapes.

He tipped them each a noble;
　　Said they, 'Tis nobly done,
We're sure your royal highness must
　　Have stopped the man in fun.

They next caught Poins, the footpad,
　　Who tipped them half a crown;
They took *it*—and in custody
　　They took *him* up to town.

That very day a learned judge
  Was seated on the bench,
Who loved a bite, and loved a sup,
  And hated not a wench.

Gascoigne, Chief Justice, was his name,
  A venerable wight,
Yclep'd from wine of Gascony,
  In which he took delight.

His judgments in the Year-books
  With profit you may read;
They're shorter than his beard—for that
  Was very long indeed.

This grave and learned justice was
  Presiding at the Bailey,
Then called the New, but now the Old,
  And growing older daily.

When Poins he spied—Ho, ho! he cried,
  The caitiff hither bring,
We'll have a quick deliverance
  Betwixt him and the king.

And sooth he said, for justice sped
  In those days at a rate,

Which now 'twere vain to seek to gain
  In matters small or great.

No tribe with rusty, camlet gowns, ·
  And shabby horsehair wigs,
Harangued the upper gallery
  In favor of the prigs.

No troops of venal witnesses,
  Inured to perjury,
Were ever brought by knaves who sought,
  To prove an alibi.
The speedy arm of Justice
  Was never known to fail;
The gaol supplied the gallows,
  The gallows thinned the gaol.
And sundry wise precautions
  The sages of the Law
Discreetly framed, whereby they aimed
  To keep the rogues in awe.
For, lest some sturdy criminal
  False witnesses should bring,
His witnesses were not allowed
  To swear to anything.
And lest his wily advocate
  8   The Court should overreach,

His advocate was not allowed
   The privilege of speech.
Yet, such was the humanity
   ·And wisdom of the Law,
That, if in his indictment there
   Appeared to be a flaw,
The Court assigned him counsellors
   To argue on the doubt,
Provided he *himself* had first
   Contrived to point it out.
Yet lest their mildness should, perchance,
   Be craftily abused,
To *show* him the indictment they
   Most sturdily refused.
But still, that he might understand
   The nature of the charge,
The same was in the Latin tongue
   Read out to him at large.
'Twas thus the law kept rogues at awe,
   Gave honest men protection,
And justly famed, by all was named,
   "*Of wisdom the perfection.*"

But now the case is different
   The rogues are getting bold—
It was not so some time ago,
   In those good days of old.

YE JUVENILE OFFENDER.

BY A PUZZLED MAGISTRATE.

FORTUNE, impartial to each dog,
  Gives a brief day of splendor;
Like favor she hath not denied
  The juvenile offender.

Perchance by some more vulgar name
  You've known this new pretender,
Ere by promotion he became
  A juvenile offender.

In face and figure immature,
  Of the superior gender,
An interesting juvenile's
  Our juvenile offender.

His age might puzzle you and me,
  For though he's small and slender,
He's always mighty wide awake,
  Our juvenile offender.

The law he breaks like any lad
  Who no account need render;

His sins are adult, though he is
    A juvenile offender.

The wise men of the land confer,
    Advice they ask and tender,
They cry, How shall we punish him,
    Our juvenile offender?

By fine? He is a juvenile,
    And not a money-spender.
Imprisonment? It might offend
    Our juvenile offender.

The birch? 'Tis clearly not the thing
    For one so young and tender;
It might degrade, or even pain,
    Our juvenile offender.

While these wise men confabulate,
    Reflection doth engender
The thought, How fine a thing to be
    A juvenile offender!

ON THE LAW OF MARRIAGE.

THOUGHTS AT SEA.

O MARRIAGE—tell me if you truly are
    A deity, as poets represent ye!
Or are you, as the Institutes declare,
    Nothing but a *consensus de presenti?*
No matter!—I espoused a maid of twenty,
By promise and a process *subsequente.*

We married without contract; but our rights
    Were all defined within the year and day.
A youngster came one o' the cold spring nights—
    I hardly had expected him till May.
My wife did well—in fact, as well as could be;
The baby squeaked, and all was as it should be.

The darling's eyes were dark and deeply set;
    My wife's and mine were light and round and full;
His hair was thick and coarse, and black as jet,
    While ours was thin and fair, and soft as wool:
I knew 'twas vain to play the rude remonstrant,
For *pater est quem nuptiæ demonstrant.*

The am'rous youth may fervidly maintain
  That marriage is a cure for every trouble;
The feudalist may learnedly explain
  When its avail is single and when double:
Its sole avail to me, I grieve to say it,
Was debt—without the wherewithal to pay it.

And debt brings duns. My dun was of a sort
  That never can desist from persecution.
He brought my case before the Sheriff Court—
  My debt, they told him, needed constitution.
'Twas false! He knew—I knew it to my curse—
It had the constitution of a horse.

But the decree went out, and I went in—
  And in the jail lived *more debitorum;*
Yet though I lost my flesh, I saved my skin
  By suing for a *cessio bonorum.*
I got out, naked as an unfurred rabbit.
The Lords dispensed, they told me, with the habit.

I went to seek my wife, but she had fled,
  And had not left a single paraphernal;
But matrimonial law upon my head
  Seemed destined still to pour its curse eternal.
I had indeed obtained a separation
From bed and board—no prospect but starvation!

But bed and board are things worth striving for,
   So I bethought me of the pea and thimble ;
But people had grown wiser than of yore,
   And all in vain I plied my fingers nimble.
I then attempted vicious intromission,
And was immediately conveyed to prison.

And here again I lay upon my oars ;
   A hermit keeps his cell—my cell kept me.
No letters came to me of open doors ;
   Criminal letters, though, came postage free.
The air I breathed just added to my cares,
Reminding me of coming Justice Ayres.

And come they did ! And therefore am I now
   Upon thy wave, old ocean, Sydney bound !
And here the partner of my youthful vow
   Among the fourteen-yearers have I found ;
Here are we (though not just as when we courted)
Again united and again transported.

THE TOURIST'S MATRIMONIAL GUIDE THROUGH SCOTLAND.

Y E tourists, who Scotland would enter,
  The summer or autumn to pass,
I'll tell you how far you may venture
  To flirt with your lad or your lass;
How close you may come upon marriage,
  Still keeping the wind of the law,
And not by some foolish miscarriage
  Get woo'd and married an' a'.
      Woo'd and married an' a';
        Married and woo'd an' a';
      And not by some foolish miscarriage
        Get woo'd and married an' a'.

This maxim itself might content ye—
  That marriage is made by consent,
Provided it's done *de præsenti*,
  And marriage is really what's meant.
Suppose that young Jocky and Jenny
  Say, " We two are husband and wife ";
The witnesses needn't be many:
  They're instantly buckled for life.

Woo'd and married an' a';
Married and woo'd an' a';
It isn't with us a hard thing
To get woo'd and married an' a'.

Suppose the man only has spoken,
The woman just given a nod,
They're spliced by that very same token,
Till one of them's under the sod.
Though words would be bolder and blunter,
The want of them isn't a flaw;
For *nutu signisque loquuntur*
Is good consistorial law.
Woo'd and married an' a';
Married and woo'd an' a';
A wink is as good as a word
To get woo'd and married an' a'.

If people are drunk or delirious,
The marriage of course would be bad;
Or if they're not sober and serious,
But acting a play or charade.
It's bad if it's only a cover
For cloaking a scandal or sin,
And talking a landlady over,
To let the folks lodge in her inn.

Woo'd and married an' a';
  Married and woo'd an' a';
It isn't the mere use of words
  Makes you woo'd and married an' a'.

You'd better keep clear of love letters,
  Or write them with caution and care;
For faith, they may fasten your fetters,
  If wearing a conjugal air.
Unless you're a knowing old stager,
  'Tis here you'll most likely be lost;
As a certain much-talked-about major
  Had very near found to his cost.
    Woo'd and married an' a';
      Married and woo'd an' a';
    They are perilous things, pen and ink,
      To get woo'd and married an' a'.

I ought now to tell the unwary
  That into the noose they'll be led,
By giving a promise to marry,
  And acting as if they were wed.
But if, when the promise you're plighting,
  To keep it you think you'd be loath,
Just see that it isn't in writing,
  And then it must come to your oath.

Woo'd and married an' a';
Married and woo'd an' a';
I've shown you a dodge to avoid
Being woo'd and married an' a'

A third way of tying the tether,
Which sometimes may happen to suit,
Is living a good while together,
And getting a married repute.
But you, who are here as a stranger,
And don't mean to stay with us long,
Are little exposed to that danger;
So here I may finish my song.
Woo'd and married an' a';
Married and woo'd an' a';
You're taught now to seek or to shun
Being woo'd and married an' a'.

THE PURCHASING OF LAND.

FIRST, see the land which thou intend'st to buy,
Within the Seller's Title clear to lie;
And that no Woman to it doth lay Claim
By Dowry, Joynture, or some other Name
That may it cumber. Know if bound or free
The Tenure stand, and that from each Feoffee
It be releas'd, That th' Seller be so old,
That he may lawful sell, thou lawful hold;
Have special care that it not Mortgag'd be,
Nor be intayled on Posterity.
Then if it stand in Statute, bound or no,
Be well advis'd what Quitrent out must go,
What Custom service hath been done of old,
By those who formerly the same did hold,
And if a wedded Woman put to Sale,
Deal not with her, unless she bring her Male;
For she doth under Covert-Baron go.
Although sometimes some traffique so (we know).
Thy Bargain being made, and all this done,
Have special care to make thy Charter run
To thee, thy Heirs, Executors, Assigns,
For that beyond thy Life, securely binds.

Those things foreknown, and done, you may prevent
Those things Rash Buyers many times repent.
And yet when you have done all that you can,
If you'll be sure, deal with an honest Man.

9

THE JOLLY TESTATOR WHO MAKES HIS OWN WILL.

AIR.—"Argyll is My Name."

YE lawyers who live upon litigants' fees,
And who need a good many to live at your ease,
Grave or gay, wise or witty, whate'er your degree,
Plain stuff or Queen's Counsel, take counsel of me.
When a festive occasion your spirit unbends,
You should never forget the profession's best
　　friends;
So we'll send round the wine, and a light bumper
　　fill
To the jolly testator who makes his own will.

He premises his wish and his purpose to save
All disputes among friends when he's laid in his
　　grave;
Then he straightway proceeds more disputes to
　　create
Than a long summer's day would give time to relate.
He writes and erases, he blunders and blots,
He produces such puzzles and Gordian knots,
That a lawyer, intending to frame the deed *ill*,
Couldn't match the testator who makes his own will.

Testators are good; but a feeling more tender
Springs up when I think of the feminine gender.
The testatrix for me, who, like Telemaque's mother,
Unweaves at one time what she wove at another.
She bequeaths, she repeats, she recalls a donation,
And she ends by revoking her own revocation;
Still scribbling or scratching some new codicil;
O, success to the woman who makes her own will!

'Tisn't easy to say, 'mid her varying vapors,
That scraps should be deemed "testamentary
    papers";
'Tisn't easy from these her intention to find,
When, perhaps, she herself never knew her own
    mind.
Every step that we take, there arises fresh trouble.
Is the legacy lapsed? is it single, or double?
No customer brings so much grist to the mill
As the wealthy old woman who makes her own
    will.

The law decides questions of *meum* and *tuum*,
By kindly consenting to make the thing *suum*.
The Æsopian fable instructively tells
What becomes of the oysters, and who gets the
    shells

The legatees starve, but the lawyers are fed ;
The seniors have riches, the juniors have bread ;
The available surplus, of course, will be *nil*
From the worthy testators who make their own will.

You had better pay toll when you take to the road
Than attempt by a by-way to reach your abode ;
You had better employ a conveyancer's hand
Than encounter the risk that your will shouldn't
         stand.
From the broad, beaten track when the traveller
         strays,
He may land in a bog or be lost in a maze ;
And the law, when defied, will avenge itself still
On the man and the woman who make their own
         will.

THE LAST WILL AND TESTAMENT OF WILLIAM RUFFELL, ESQ.

As this life must soon end, and my frame will decay,
And my soul to some far-distant clime wing its way,
Ere that time arrives, now I free am from cares,
I thus wish to settle my worldly affairs—
A course right and proper men of sense will agree.
I am now strong and hearty, my age forty-three;
I make this my last will, as I think 'tis quite time,
It conveys all I wish, though 'tis written in rhyme,
To employ an attorney I ne'er was inclin'd,
They are pests to society, sharks of mankind.
To avoid that base tribe my own will I now draw,
May I ever escape coming under their paw.
To Ezra Dalton, my nephew, I give all my land,
With the old Gothic cottage that thereon doth
    stand;
'Tis near Shimpling great road, in which I now
    dwell,
It looks like a chapel or hermit's old cell,
With my furniture, plate, and linen likewise,
And securities, money, with what may arise.
'Tis my wish and desire that he should enjoy these,
And pray let him take even my skin, if he please.

To my loving, kind sister I give and bequeath,
For her tender regard, when this world I shall
    leave,
If she choose to accept it, my rump-bone may
    take,
And tip it with silver, a whistle to make.
My brother-in-law is a strange-tempered dog;
He's as fierce as a tiger, in manners a hog;
A petty tyrant at home, his frowns how they dread;
Two ideas at once never entered his head.
So proud and so covetous, moreover so mean,
I dislike to look at him, the fellow is so lean.
He ne'er behaved well, and, though very unwilling,
Yet I feel that I must cut him off with a shilling.
My executors, too, should be men of good fame;
I appoint Edmund Ruffell, of Cockfield, by name;
In his old easy-chair, with short pipe and snuff,
What matter his whims, he is honest enough;
With Samuel Seely, of Alpheton Lion,
I like his strong beer, and his word can rely on.
When Death's iron hand gives the last fatal blow,
And my shattered old frame in the dust must lie
    low,
Without funeral pomp let my remains be conveyed
To Brent Eleigh churchyard, near my father be
    laid.

This, written with my own hand, there can be no
    appeal,
I now therefore at once set my hand and my seal,
As being my last will; I to this fully agree,
This eighteenth day of March, eighteen hundred
    and three.

A LAWYER'S WILL.

This is my last Will and Testament:
Read it according to my intent.
My gracious God to me hath giv'n
Store of good things that, under heav'n,
Are giv'n to those "that love the Lord,
And hear and do his sacred word":
I therefore give to my dear wife
All my estates, to keep for life,
Real and personal, profits, rents,
Messuages, lands, and tenements;
After her death I give the whole
Unto my children, one and all,
To take as "Tenants in Common" do,
Not as "Joint Tenants," *per mie, per tout.*
I give "all my Trust Estates" in fee
To Charlotte, my wife and devisee,
To hold to her, on trust, the same
As I now hold them in my name;
I give her power to convey the fee
As fully as though 'twere done by me,
And here declare that from all charges,
My wife's "receipts are good discharges."

May God Almighty bless his Word
To all "my presents from the Lord,"
May he his blessings on them shed
When down in sleep they lay their head.
And now, my wife, my hopes I fix
On thee, my sole executrix—
My truest, best, and to the end,
My faithful partner, "crown," and friend.

In witness thereof, I hereunto
   My hand and seal have set,
In presence of those whose names below
   Subscribe and witness it.

J. C. G.   [L. S.]

26th January, 1835.

This will was publish'd, seal'd, and sign'd
By the testator, in his right mind,
In presence of us, who, at his request,
Have written our names these facts to attest.

J. M.
D. E.
J. G. D.
Solicitors.

THE WILL OF JOSHUA WEST.

PERHAPS I died not worth a groat;
    But should I die worth something more,
Then I give that, and my best coat,
    And all my manuscripts in store,
To those who shall the goodness have
    To cause my poor remains to rest
Within a decent shell and grave.
    This is the will of Joshua West.

JOSHUA WEST.

Witnessed, R. MILLS.
        J. A. BERRY.
        JOHN BAINES.

THE WILL OF JAMES BIGSBY.

As I feel very queer, my will I now make;
Write it down, Joseph Finch, and make no mis-
    take.
I wish to leave all things fair and right, do you see,
And my relatives satisfy. Now, listen to me.
The first in my will is Lydia my wife,
Who to me proved a comfort three years of my life;
The second my poor aged mother I say,
With whom I have quarrelled on many a day,
For which I've been sorry, and also am still;
I wish to give her a place in my will.
The third that I mention is my dear little child;
When I think of her, Joseph, I feel almost wild.
Uncle Sam Bigsby, I must think of him too,
Peradventure he will say that I scarcely can do.
And poor Uncle Gregory, I must leave him a part
If it is nothing else but the back of the cart.
And for you, my executor, I will do what I can,
For acting towards me like an honest young man.

Now, to my wife I bequeath greater part of my
    store ;
First thing is the bedstead before the front door;

The next is the chair standing by the fireside,
The fender and irons she cleaned with much pride.
I also bequeath to Lydia my wife
A box in the cupboard, a sword, gun, and knife,
And the harmless old pistol without any lock,
Which no man can fire off, for 'tis minus a cock.
The cups and the saucers I leave her also,
And a book called *The History of Poor Little Mo*,
With the kettle, the boiler, and old frying-pan,
A shovel, a mud-scoop, a pail, and a pan.
And remember, I firmly declare and protest
That my poor aged mother shall have my oak chest
And the broken whip under it.   Do you hear what
   I say?
Write all these things down without any delay.
And my dear little child, I must think of her too.
Friend Joseph, I am dying, what shall I do?
I give her my banyan, my cap, and my hose,
My big monkey-jacket, my shirt, and my shoes;
And to Uncle Sam Bigsby I bequeath my high
   boots,
And pickaxe and mattock with which I stubbed
   roots.
And poor Uncle Gregory, with the whole of my
   heart,
I give for a bedstead the back of the cart.

And to you, my executor, last in my will,
I bequeath a few trifles to pay off your b.ll.
I give you my shot-belt, my dog, and my nets,
And the rest of my goods sell to pay off my debts.

JOSEPH FINCH, Executer.

Dated February 4th, 1839

10

WILLS WITHOUT LAWYERS.

Vide, " Home-made Wills."—*Newspaper Paragraph.*

I was a dissolute young blade,
 A scape-grace of the worst degree,
And so my slow old uncle made
 A will to disinherit me.

To save the lawyer's fees intent,
 The deed himself he needs must draw;
And by that precious testament,
 He cut me off—his heir-at-law.

At last the old curmudgeon died,
 And lo! the will, when 'twas perused,
Proved only signed on its outside;
 And so the probate was refused.

The tin is mine instead of Bill's,
 Although I am a worthless whelp:
So here's success to all whose wills
 Are made without a lawyer's help.

MAKE THY WILL.

O LOVE, what life shines through thine eyes
    So bright, of clear unclouded blue!
What radiant health, my treasure, dyes
    Thy dimpled cheeks with roseate hue!
How frail a thing is yet that life!
    I think its loss myself would kill;
But lest I should, my little wife,
    Perchance survive thee, make thy will.

O'er us, united, many years,
    I trust, there are to roll away;
But who can, in this vale of tears,
    Be certain of another day?
The least delay how oft we rue!
    Precaution let that thought instill,
What should be done at once to do;
    Now that is, dearest, make thy will.

Else I should not obtain the whole—
    Some part would go away from me—
My own one, make me, then, thy sole
    Executor and legatee.

Then let the happy moments fly,
  Far distant be that hour, until,
If I be not the first to die,
  When thou wilt leave me.   Make thy will.

A QUESTION OF TESTAMENTARY IN-
TERPRETATION.

A ROMAN lawyer, as the story goes,
A question of this kind did first propose:
That if a person die and leave behind
His whole estate—the amount is here subjoined,
    8,000*l*—
And wife with child, then 'tis his will and mind,
That of a son she should deliver'd be,
Two-thirds must be his share, one-third for she;
But if a daughter, then the widow's share
Must be two-thirds, the daughter one-third clear,
Now, soon the widow is, as we do say,
Delivered of a daughter and a boy;
Now, to answer the father's will, come tell to me,
How the estate (with justice) must divided be.

ANSWER.

Unto the Roman lawyer thus I say,
In answer to his " moot point" rais'd to-day;
Whereas, the father (the testator) died,
And for the event, that chanc'd fail'd to provide,
And " Justice " thus was left (alas!) to find
And to discover how the father, kind

(Had he but thought), would have express'd his
      mind;
It seems but right (to me, at least) to say,
One-half the amount the executor should pay
Unto the son; the daughter and her mother
Taking in equal moieties the other.

CANONS OF DESCENT.

CANON I.

ESTATES go to the issue (*item*)
Of him last seized, *in infinitum ;*
Like cow tails, downward straight they tend,
But never lineally ascend;

CANON II.

This gives that preference to males,
At which a lady justly rails;

CANON III.

Of two males in the same degree
The eldest, only, heir shall be ;
With females we this order break,
And let them altogether take :

CANON IV.

When one his worldly strife hath ended,
Those who are lineally descended
From him, as to his claims and riches,
Shall stand precisely in his breeches;

CANON V.

When lineal descendants fail,
Collaterals the land may nail;
So that they be (and that a bore is)
De sanguine progenitoris.

CANON VI.

The heir collateral, d'ye see,
Next kinsman of whole blood must be;

CANON VII.

And of collaterals, the male
Stocks are preferred to female,
Unless the land come from the woman,
And then her heirs shall yield to no man.

RULES OF DESCENT IN THE UNITED STATES.

AS LAID DOWN BY KENT IN 1831.

If one dies owning an estate
It lineally must gravitate;
If but one heir it will annex,
To him or her in spite of sex;
If there be more, as well there may,
They all shall take *per capita.*

But if degrees, perchance, there be,
Of different consanguinity,
As sons and grandsons, all shall take,
And an estate in common make;
But such grandsons have cause to fear it.
They'll not an item more inherit,
Than would have been their father's share,
Had he been the living heir.

But if the owner meets his fate—
No lineal heir to his estate;
We've dared the Common Law to mend
And his estate shall now ascend.

Again: in case the owner do
Lack issue and lack parents too,
His brothers and his sisters shall
Succeed by rules collateral.
If brothers, sisters, nephews, nieces,
They then will take in equal pieces;
If some be dead, some living be,
They'll take by nearness of degree.

And in default of father, mother,
And nephews, nieces, sisters, brother,
Or issue, the estate can't fall,
But yet it will rise above them all.

Again: and if perchance there shall
Be no descendants lineal—
If parents, brothers, sisters, none,
With their descendants 'neath the sun,
Nor the grandparents, the estate
Shall by unerring, legal fate
Unto the aunts and uncles wend,
And those who from them may descend;
If equally related, they
Will take their part *per capita;*
But if in different degrees,
They all shall then take per " stirpes."

Provided, if the intestate had
Derived his living from his dad,
It shall to aunts and uncles slide,
And issue on the father's side ;
And if none such there be, perchance,
Then to the uncles and the aunts
On the maternal side 'twill go ;
And this rule works *e converso.*

This eighth last rule, it seems to me,
Is rather stiff for poetry.

VARIATION OF THE RULE IN SHELLEY'S CASE.

At York, Pennsylvania, recently died
A gentleman who, in his life-time, was tied
With bonds matrimonial unto a wife;
The reason, perhaps, he departed this life.

While living, however—though but a brief space
Ere departing—he had the misfortune to place
His wife in that rather peculiar position
She ne'er could have entered of her sole volition;
Then, feeling himself quite exhausted and ill,
He drew up and signed, sealed, and published his
     will,
In which, with commendable care, he provided
That at his demise his estate be divided
'Twixt his wife, soon to be a young widow forlorn,
And the child that he hoped would duly be born;
Said child, if a girl, to take only one-third;
But two-thirds, if a boy: whence it may be averred
The testator a boy to a girl much preferred.

His affairs thus arranged and his wife in said fix,
This father expectant crossed over the Styx.

Now, one would suppose—at least, at first thought,
No will could be simpler and plainer—that naught
Could, by any contingency, happen to throw
Any doubt as to how the estate was to go:
To the widow, one-third, or two-thirds, or the whole,
As the issue might be and the embryo soul
Prove a male or a female, or perish at birth ;
To the child, if a girl it should happen to be,
One-third; if a boy, then two parts out of three.
Was ever a more simple will made on earth ?

But (to alter a proverb Française),
L'homme propose, la femme dispose.   Nine months
   to a day,
After shrouding her husband, our widow began
To put into bold execution a plan
She'd conceived with intent to demolish completely
The will the deceased thought he'd drawn up so
   neatly.
She sent for a priest and confessed all her sins,
Then took to her bed and gave birth to—twins;
And, as if her dead lord to spite doubly, and vex
   his
Pale ghost, *the said twins were of opposite sexes !*

And now all the lawyers and judges and friends
Of this troublesome widow are at their wit's ends

To determine just how the estate to divide ;
And they find it a right knotty point to decide:
Shall the boy have two-thirds while the other third
      goes
To the girl, and the widow get naught for her
      throes?
Or must we allow the astute widow's claim
To two-thirds on the plea that a feminine came,
And to one-third beside on the opposite plea
That one of the posthumous heirs is a *he?*
Or shall the whole go to the lawyers and court?
Or where else must a fitting solution be sought?
'Tis a question o'er which it will be easy to quarrel,
Let us leave it unanswered and draw a brief moral.

MORAL.

Ye over-affectionate husbands, take care !
Not to leave *twins* behind you in *ventre sa mere.*
Above all, harbor not the preposterous thought,
Your will can your widow's will possibly thwart.

ST. PETER *VS.* A LAWYER.

PROFESSIONS will abuse each other;
The priest won't call the lawyer brother,
While *Salkeld* still beknaves the parson,
And says he cants to keep the farce on.
Yet will I readily suppose
They are not truly bitter foes,
But only have their pleasant jokes,
And banter, just like other folks.
As thus, for so they quiz the Law,
Once on a time, the attorney, Flaw.
A man, to tell you as the fact is,
Of vast chicane, of course of practice
(But what profession can we trace
Where some will not the corps disgrace?
Seduc'd, perhaps, by roguish client,
Who tempt him to become more pliant),
A notice had to quit the world,
And from his desk at once was hurl'd.
Observe, I pray, the plain narration :
'Twas in a hot and long vacation,
When time he had, but no assistance,
Though great from courts of law the distance,

To reach the court of truth and justice
(Where I confess, my only trust is),
Though here below the learned pleader
Shows talents worthy of a leader,
Yet his own fame he must support,
Be sometimes witty with the court,
Or work the passions of a jury
By tender strains, or, full of fury,
Mislead them all, tho' twelve apostles,
While with the new law the judge he jostles,
And makes them all give up their pow'rs,
To speeches of at least three hours.
But we have left our little man,
And wander'd from our purpos'd plan:
'Tis said (without ill-natured leaven),
If ever lawyers get to heaven,
It surely is by slow degrees
(Perhaps 'tis slow they take their fees).
The case then, now, I fairly state:
Flaw reach'd at last to heaven's high gate:
Quite short he rapp'd, none did it neater,
The gate was open'd by St. Peter,
Who look'd astonish'd when he saw
All black, the little man of law;
But Charity was Peter's guide,
For having once himself denied

His Master, he would not o'erpass
The penitent of any class;
Yet having never heard there enter'd
A lawyer, nay, nor one that ventur'd
Within the realms of peace and love,
He told him, mildly, to remove,
And would have clos'd the gate of day,
Had not old Flaw, in suppliant way,
Demurring to so hard a fate,
Begg'd but a look, tho', through the gate.
St. Peter, rather off his guard,
Unwilling to be thought too hard,
Opens the gate to let him peep in.
What did the lawyer? Did he creep in?
Or dash at once to take possession?
O no; he knew his own profession;
He took his hat off with respect,
And would no gentle means neglect;
But finding it was all in vain
For him admittance to obtain,
Thought it were best, let come what will,
To gain an entry by his skill.
So while St. Peter stood aside
To let the door be open'd wide,
He skimm'd his hat with all his strength
Within the gate to no small length:

St. Peter star'd ; the lawyer asked him,
" Only to fetch his hat," and pass'd him,
But when he reach'd the jack he'd thrown,
O, then was all the lawyer shown;
He clapp'd it on, and arms a-kembo
(As if he'd been the gallant *Bembo*),
Cry'd out, " What think you of my plan ?
Eject me, Peter, if you can."

JUSTICE AND THE LAWYER.

Past twelve o'clock, the watchman cry'd;
His brief the studious lawyer plied;
The all-prevailing fee lay nigh,
The earnest of to-morrow's lie.
Sudden the furious winds arise,
The jarring casement shatter'd flies;
The doors admit a hollow sound,
And rattling from their hinges bound,
When Justice, in a blaze of light,
Reveal'd her radiant form to sight.

The wretch with thrilling horror shook,
Loose every joint, and pale his look;
Not having seen her in the courts,
Or found her mentioned in reports,
He ask'd, with falt'ring tongue, her name,
Her errand there, and whence she came.

Sternly the white-rob'd shade reply'd,
(A crimson glow her visage dy'd),
Canst thou be doubtful who I am?
Is Justice grown so strange a name?
Were not your courts for Justice rais'd?
'Twas there of old my altars blaz'd.

My guardian thee I did elect,
My sacred temple to protect.
That thou and all thy venal tribe
Should spurn the goddess for the bribe!
Aloud the ruin'd client cries
That Justice has nor ears nor eyes;
In foul alliance with the bar,
'Gainst me the judge denounces war,
And rarely issues his decree
But with intent to baffle me.

She paus'd.   Her breast with fury burn'd.
The trembling lawyer thus return'd:

I own the charge is justly laid,
And weak th' excuse that can be made;
Yet search the spacious globe and see
If all mankind are not like me.
The gownsman, skilled in Romish lies,
By faith's false glass deludes our eyes;
O'er conscience rides, without control,
And robs the man to save his soul.
The doctor, with important face,
By sly design mistakes the case;
Prescribes, and spies out the disease,
To trick the patient of his fees.

The soldier, rough with many a scar,
And red with slaughter, leads the war;
If he a nation's trust betray,
The foe has offered double pay.
When vice o'er all mankind prevails,
And weighty interest turns the scales,
Must I be better than the rest,
And harbor justice in my breast?
On one side only take the fee,
Content with poverty and thee?

Thou blind to sense, and vile of mind,
The exasperated shade rejoin'd,
If virtue from the world is flown,
Will others' faults excuse thy own?
For sickly souls the first was made;
Physicians for the body's aid;
The soldier guarded liberty;
Man, woman, and the lawyer me.
If all are faithless to their trust,
They leave not thee the less unjust.
Henceforth your pleadings I disclaim,
And bar the sanction of my name;
Within your courts it shall be read,
That Justice from the law is fled.

THE DEVIL AND THE LAWYERS.

THE Devil came up to the earth one day,
And into the court he wended his way,
Just as the attorney, with very grave face,
Was proceeding to argue the point in a case.

Now, a lawyer his majesty never had seen;
For to his dominions none ever had been,
And he felt very anxious the reason to know
Why none had been sent to the regions below.

'Twas the fault of his agents, his majesty thought,
That none of these lawyers had ever been caught!
And for his own pleasure he felt a desire
To come to the earth and the reason inquire.

Well, the lawyer who rose, with a visage so grave
Made out his opponent a consummate knave;
And Satan felt considerably amused
To hear the attorney so badly abused.

But soon as the speaker had come to a close,
The counsel opposing him fiercely arose,
And heaped such abuse on the head of the first,
That made him a villain of all men the worst.

Thus they quarrelled, contended, and argued so long,
'Twas hard to determine which of them was wrong,
And concluding he'd heard enough of the fuss,
Old Nick turned away, and soliloquized thus:

"They've puzzled the court with their villainous
      cavil,
And, I'm free to confess it, they've puzzled the Devil.
My agents were right to let lawyers alone,
If I had them they'd swindle me out of my throne."

THE FARMER AND THE COUNSELLOR.

A COUNSEL in the Common Pleas
Who was esteemed a mighty wit,
Upon the strength of a chance hit
Amid a thousand flippancies,
And his occasional bad jokes
In bullying, bantering, brow-beating,
Ridiculing and maltreating
Women, or other timid folks,
In a late cause resolved to hoax
A clownish Yorkshire farmer—one
Who, by his uncouth look and gait,
Appear'd expressly meant by Fate
For being quizz'd and play'd upon.
So having tipp'd the wink to those
    In the back rows,
Who kept their laughter bottled down
Until our wag should draw the cork,
He smiled jocosely on the clown,
    And went to work.
" Well, Farmer Numskull, how go
    Calves at York ? "
" Why—not, sir, as they do wi' you,
But on four legs instead of two."

"Officer!" cried the legal elf,
Piqued at the laugh against himself,
"Do, pray, keep silence down below there:
Now look at me, clown, attend,
Have I not seen you somewhere, friend?"
"Yees—very like—I often go there."
"Our rustic's waggish, quite laconic,"
The counsel cried, with grin sardonic;
"I wish I'd known this prodigy,
This genius of the clods, when I
On circuit was at York residing.
Now, farmer, do for once speak true,
Mind, you're on oath, so tell me, you
Who doubtless think yourself so clever,
Are there as many fools as ever
     In the West Riding?"
"Why, no, sir, no; we've got our share,
But not so many as when you were there."

12

THE COUNSEL'S TEAR.

If Faraday's or Liebig's art
 Could crystallize this legal treasure,
Long might a pleader near his heart
 The jewel wear with chuckling pleasure.

The native brilliant, ere it fell,
 A squeeze produced in Walker's eye,
Which, winking, dropped the liquid "sell,"
 The spring of plausibility.

Nice drop of rich and racy light,
 In thee the rays of Humor shine;
Almost as queer, all but as bright,
 As any gem or joke of mine.

Thou fine effusion of the soul!
 That never fail'st to gain relief,
Which barristers can ne'er control,
 When thou art like to help their brief:

The farce-wright's and the jester's theme,
 In many a joke, on many a stage,
Thou moisten'st Chitty's arid theme,
 And Blackstone's dry and dreary page.

That very lawyer who a tear
    Can shed, as from the bosom's source,
With feeling equally sincere,
    Could weep on t'other side—of course.

BAINES CAREW, GENTLEMAN.

Of all the good attorneys who
    Have placed their names upon the roll,
But few could equal Baines Carew
    For tender-heartedness and soul.

Whene'er he heard a tale of woe
    From client A or client B,
His grief would overcome him so
    He'd scarce have strength to take his fee.

It laid him up for many days,
    When duty led him to distrain;
And serving writs, although it pays,
    Gave him excruciating pain.

He made out costs, distrained for rent,
    Foreclosed and sued, with moistened eye—
No bill of costs could represent
    The value of such sympathy.

No charges can approximate
    The worth of sympathy with woe;—
Although I think I ought to state
    He did his best to make them so.

Of all the many clients who
   Had mustered round his legal flag,
No single client of the crew
   Was half so dear as CAPTAIN BAGG.

Now, CAPTAIN BAGG had bowed him to
   A heavy matrimonial yoke—
His wifey had of faults a few—
   She never could resist a joke.

Her chaff at first he meekly bore,
   Till unendurable it grew.
" To stop this persecution sore
   I will consult my friend CAREW.

" And when CAREW's advice I've got,
   Divorce *a mensâ* I shall try."
(A legal separation—not
   A vinculo conjugii.)

" O, BAINES CAREW, my woe I've kept
   A secret hitherto, you know ";—
(And BAINES CAREW, ESQUIRE, he wept
   To hear that BAGG *had* any woe.)

" My case, indeed, is passing sad.
   My wife—whom I considered true—
With brutal conduct drives me mad."
   " I am appalled," said BAINES CAREW.

" What! sound the matrimonial knell
    Of worthy people such as these!
Why was I an attorney? Well—
    Go on to the *sævitia*, please."

" Domestic bliss has proved my bane—
    A harder case you never heard,
My wife (in other matters sane)
    Pretends that I'm a Dicky bird!

" She makes me sing, 'Too-whit, too-wee!'
    And stand upon a rounded stick,
And always introduces me
    To every one as 'Pretty Dick'!"

" O, dear," said weeping BAINES CAREW,
    " This is the direst case I know."
" I'm grieved," said BAGG, " at paining you—
    To COBB & POLTHERTHWAITE I'll go—

" To COBB's cold, calculating ear,
    My grewsome sorrows I'll impart "—
" No; stop," said BAINES, " I'll dry my tear,
    And steel my sympathetic heart."

" She makes me perch upon a tree,
    Rewarding me with 'Sweety—nice!'
And threatens to exhibit me
    With four or five performing mice."

"Restrain my tears I wish I could"
  (Said BAINES), "I don't know what to do."
Said CAPTAIN BAGG, "You're very good."
  "O, not at all," said BAINES CAREW.

"She makes me fire a gun," said BAGG;
  "And, at a preconcerted word,
Climb up a ladder with a flag,
  Like any street performing bird.

"She places sugar in my way—
  In public places calls me 'Sweet!'
She gives me groundsel every day,
  And hard canary-seed to eat."

"Oh, woe! oh, sad! oh, dire to tell!"
  (Said BAINES).   "Be good enough to stop."
And senseless on the floor he fell,
  With unpremeditated flop.

Said CAPTAIN BAGG, "Well, really I
  Am grieved to think it pains you so.
I thank you for your sympathy;
  But, hang it!—come—I say, you know!"

But BAINES lay flat upon the floor,
  Convulsed with sympathetic sob;—
The Captain toddled off next door,
  And gave the case to MR. COBB.

POOR RICHARD'S OPINION.

I know you lawyers can with ease
Twist words and meanings as you please;
That language, by your skill made pliant,
Will bend, to favor every client;
That 'tis the fee limits the sense
To make out either side's pretense,
When you peruse the clearest case,
You see it with a double face,
For skepticism's your profession,
You hold there's doubt in all expression.

Hence is the Bar with fees supplied,
Hence eloquence takes either side;
Your hand would have but paltry gleaning
Could every man express his meaning.
Who dares presume to pen a deed
Unless you previously are feed?
'Tis drawn, and *to augment the cost*,
In dull prolixity engrossed;
And now we're well secured by law,
Till the next brother find a flaw.

THE RUSH TO THE BAR.

Air.—" The Low-backed Car."

Now listen, and I'll sing you
  Some light and artless rhymes,
We need such lays our hearts to raise,
  In these distressful times.
The song that I will sing you
  Is not of deeds of war,
But about the lads that come in squads,
  To join the Scottish Bar.
Chorus: To enter the ranks of the Bar,
    They are flocking from near and far!
    I think they are mad, but still I am glad
    That there should be such faith in the Bar.

No year that we remember,
  Such a crop of them has seen,
There have passed since last December,
  Not less than *seventeen !*
And *eight* have paid their entrance fees,
  Who'll pass, no doubt, next year,
To walk the boards, and increase the hoards,
  The widow's souls that cheer.

Chorus: Such a rush as there is to the Bar,
             In spite of hard times and war!
             Their wigs when they don, I hope they'll
                 get on,
             And be pleased that they came to the Bar.

        To us behind the scenes here,
            The sight seems rather strange;
        For trade is slack, though there's no lack
            Of movement and of change;
        Our prizes are not many,
            And when a chance we see,
        The question now seems always how
            That they may best abolished be!
Chorus: But yet they come on to the Bar,
             Each hoping to prove a star,
             The places to fill, that are vacant still,
             Of the former great lights of the Bar.

        To the learned Examinators
            You'll justice do, I'm sure,
        Their work has been, as you may ween,
            This year no sinecure.
        'Tis reckoned a proof of vigor
            To yield at a birth two or more;
        But what will you say when in one day
            Our Faculty brought forth Four!

Chorus : Thus we keep up the life of the Bar,
　　　　　And from dread of extinction are far!
　　　　　While promising boys come to add to our
　　　　　　joys,
　　　　　And share in the luck of the Bar.

Then pledge the bold young jurists
　　Who have joined our ranks this year;
Their healths we'll drink, whatever we think
　　Of the folly that brings them here.
I hope they have private fortunes,
　　To furnish the sinews of war ;
If not, let us pray, they never may say,
　　We were daft when we thought of the Bar.

Chorus : So let them come on to the Bar,
　　　　　Things can scarcely be worse than they
　　　　　　are!
　　　　　Here's success to the lads, who are com-
　　　　　　ing in squads
　　　　　To prove that there's life in the Bar!

THE SONG OF THE INTRANT.

" Vos lucernas juris nocturnâ versate mann, versate diurnâ."

WITH eyelids heavy and red,
  Intent on the labor of cram,
An Intrant sat, with dishevelledhair,
  Preparing for his Exam.
Read, read, read!
  Morning, noon, and night;
And still at his books, without liquor or weed,
  He sat till early light!

Read, read, read!
  While the cabs go rattling past;
And read, read, read!
  Till the gay world's home at last.
It's oh! to be at the Ball,
  With its dance, flirtation, and " cham,"
The cool walk home, the quiet cigar—
  Confound this horrid Exam.!

Read, read, read!
  Till the brain begins to swim;
Read, read, read!
  Till the eyes are heavy and dim.

Stair, Erskine, and Hume,
　　Hume, Erskine, and Stair,
Till over the volumes I sleepily nod,
　　And headlong descend from my chair!

Grind, grind, grind!
　　My brain I never rest!
And for what?　Perhaps a petition or two,
　　With a jury trial at best!
The Bar is waxing large,
　　The causes are waxing few ;
Naught but a briefless life stands out
　　To my despairing view!

Read, read, read!
　　From weary chime to chime ;
Read, read, read!
　　As prisoners work for crime!
Bell and Menzies and Ross,
　　Ross, Menzies, and Bell,
Till the head grows hot and the feet grow cold,
　　And the veins of the temples swell.

Read, read, read!
　　In the dull December light ;

13

And read, read, read!
    When the weather is warm and bright.
I daren't go down to golf,
    Cricket I must forswear,
Basket and rod must be laid on the shelf,
    There isn't a day to spare.

Oh! but to breathe the breath
    Of the cowslip and primrose sweet,
With the sky above my head,
    And the grass beneath my feet!
Though for cowslip and primrose and grass
    I did not care one straw,
Before in an evil hour I resolved
    To begin the study of law.

Oh! but for one short hour!
    A respite however short!
A little leisure to walk or ride,
    If I haven't the time for sport.
A two hours' ride would freshen me up,
    And yet I must toil on here
Till my temples throb and my sight grows dim,
    And my head feels dull and queer!

With shoulders weary and bent,
    Unflaggingly striving to cram,

An Intrant sat with an aching head
   Preparing for his Exam.
Read, read, read,
   From eve till early light,
And still of the hours he took no heed
He rested neither to sleep nor feed,
   But sat there day and night!

CROSSING THE RUBICON.

Despite of a little fear lurking,
    I have pulled through my final Exam.;
So adieu for a short time to working,
    And farewell forever to cram.
I shall put on my gown—not unheeded;
    Some, seniors, shall wish me good luck,
Will tell me of men who've succeeded—
    Not a word about those who have stuck.

In this breathing space, just for a moment
    I brood, and I muse, and inquire
What my fortune is—well or ill omened?
    What my portion is—lower or higher?
Come, tell me, thou ancient *haruspex,*
    Are we classed with the fortunate few?
Shall sunshine or shade rest on us specks
    Of cloud in the infinite blue?

Shall the barque of my fortunes, a " clean ship,"
    Return to the port whence it came?
May I ever aspire to the Deanship
    And to leaving a notable name?
Shall I come to be Lord Justice-General,
    Or only be Lord Justice Clerk?

Comes a sinister whisper, "New men are all
    Inclined to shoot over the mark."

Shall I rank with the forcible-feebles,
    Or shall I come out as a star?
Shall I try salmon fishers in Peebles,
    Preferring that much to the bar?
Shall I, waft on a wild wind, be borne away
    To regions forlorn and remote?
To Lerwick, Lochmaddy, or Stornoway,
    Where life is not worth half a groat?

After years shall I willingly take a
    Decent banishment out in Ceylon,
Judge coolies and blacks in Jamaica,
    Or elsewhere in some tropical zone?
On the Gold Coast, o'er niggers and kroomen,
    Shall it be my sad fortune to reign?
Notâ bene, some good men and true men
    Such little jobs did not disdain.

Or tied to the helm of some journal,
    Shall I drudge through the sultry July,
And feel it not easy to spurn all
    Temptations to have a "good shy"?
Let the high fates our fortunes determine,
    Yet what matters their smile or their frown?
Some hearts have been sad 'neath the ermine
    That were merry beneath the stuff gown.

I own, like the rest of mankind, most
  Legal folks rather favor the first;
So with watch-word of "Deuce take the hindmost!"
  Let us go at our work with a burst.
Nay! nay! with an honest endeavor,
  With a spirit that's gallant and true,
Let us strive and be thankful—whatever
  The fates bring to me and to you.

ADVICE TO A YOUNG LAWYER.

Whene'er you speak, remember every cause
Stands not on eloquence, but stands on laws;
Pregnant in matter, in expression brief,
Let every sentence stand with bold relief;
On trifling points, nor time nor talents waste,
A sad offense to learning and to taste;
Nor deal with pompous phrase, nor e'er suppose
Poetic flights belong to reasoning prose;
Loose declamation may deceive the crowd,
And seem more striking as it grows more loud;
But sober sense rejects it with disdain,
As naught but empty noise, and weak as vain.
The froth of words, the school-boy's vain parade
Of books and cases—all his stock in trade—
The pert conceits, the cunning tricks and play
Of low attorneys, strung in long array,
The unseemly jest, the petulant reply,
That chatters on, and cares not how or why,
Studious, avoid unworthy themes to scan,
They sink the Speaker and disgrace the Man.
Like the false lights by flying shadows cast,
Scarce seen when present, and forgot when past.

Begin with dignity; expound with grace
Each ground of reasoning in its time and place;
Let order reign throughout; each topic touch,
Nor urge its power too little or too much,
Give each strong thought its most attractive view,
In diction clear, and yet severely true.
And, as the arguments in splendor grow,
Let each reflect its light on all below.
When to the close arrived, make no delays
By petty flourishes or verbal plays,
But sum the whole in one deep, solemn strain,
Like a strong current hastening to the main.

Be brief, be pointed; let your matter stand
Lucid in order, solid, and at hand;
Spend not your words on trifles, but condense;
Strike with the mass of thought, not drops of sense;
Press to the close with vigor, once begun;
And leave (how hard the task!)—leave off when
        done.
Who draws a labored length of reasoning out,
Puts straws in line for winds to whirl about,
Who drawls a tedious tale of learning o'er
Counts but the sands on ocean's boundless shore.
Victory in law is gain'd, as battles fought,
Not by the numbers, but the forces brought.

What boots success in skirmish or in fray,
If rout and ruin following close the day?
What worth a hundred posts maintained with skill,
If, these all held, the foe is victor still?
He who would win his cause, with power must
      frame
Points of support, and look with steady aim;
Attack the weak, defend the strong with art,
Strike but few blows, but strike them to the heart;
All scatter'd fires but end in smoke and noise,
The scorn of men, the idle play of boys.
Keep, then, this first great precept ever near:
Short be your speech, your matter strong and clear,
Earnest your manner, warm and rich your style,
Severe in taste, yet full of grace the while;
So may you reach the loftiest heights of fame,
And leave, when life is past, a deathless name.

LINES WRITTEN ON HEARING AN ARGUMENT IN COURT.

SPARE me quotations, which, tho' learn'd, are long,
On points remote at best, and rarely strong;
How sad to find our time consumed by speech,
Feeble in logic, feebler still in reach,
Yet urged in words of high and bold pretense,
As if the sound made up the lack of sense.
O, could but lawyers know the great relief,
When reasoning comes close, pointed, clear, and
　　brief;
When every sentence tells, and as it falls
With ponderous weight, renew'd attention calls—
Grave and more grave each topic, and its force
Exhausted not till ends the destined course—
Sure is the victory, if the cause be right;
If not, enough the glory of the fight.

THE BRIEFLESS BARRISTER.

A BALLAD.

An Attorney was taking a turn,
   In shabby habiliments drest;
His coat, it was shockingly worn,
   And the rust had invested his vest.

His breeches had suffered a breach,
   His linen and worsted were worse;
He had scarce a whole crown in his hat,
   And not half a crown in his purse.

And thus as he wandered along,
   A cheerless and comfortless elf,
He sought for relief in a song,
   Or complainingly talked to himself :—

"Unfortunate man that I am !
   I've never a client but grief :
The case is, I've no case at all,
   And in brief, I've ne'er had a brief !

"I've waited and waited in vain,
   Expecting an 'opening' to find,

Where an honest young lawyer might gain
　　Some reward for toil of his mind.

"'Tis not that I'm wanting in law,
　　Or lack an intelligent face,
That others have cases to plead,
　　While I have to plead for a case.

"O, how can a modest young man
　　E'er hope for the smallest progression—
The profession's already so full
　　Of lawyers so full of profession!"

While thus he was strolling around,
　　His eye accidentally fell
On a very deep hole in the ground,
　　And he sighed to himself, "It is well!"

To curb his emotions, he sat
　　On the curbstone the space of a minute,
Then cried, "Here's an opening at last!"
　　And in less than a jiffy was in it!

Next morning twelve citizens came
　　('Twas the coroner bade them attend),
To the end that it might be determined
　　How the man had determined his end!

" The man was a lawyer, I hear,"
  Quoth the foreman who sat on the corse.
" A lawyer? Alas!" said another,
  " Undoubtedly died of remorse!"

A third said, " He knew the deceased,
  An attorney well versed in the laws,
And as to the cause of his death,
  'Twas no doubt for the want of a cause."

The jury decided at length,
  After solemnly weighing the matter,
That the lawyer was drownded, because
  He could not keep his head above water.

14

ELEGY WRITTEN IN THE TEMPLE GARDENS.

The gard'ner rings the bell at close of day,
　The motley crowd wind slowly home to tea ;
Soft on the Thames the daylight fades away,
　And leaves the walks to darkness and to me.

Now shine the glimmering gas-lamps on the sight,
　The wardens now the outer portals lock,
And deepest stillness marks th' approach of night,
　Save when the watchman calls, "Past ten o'clock."

Save, also, when from yonder antique tower,[1]
　With solemn sound the bell strikes on the ear,
And wand'ring damsels, as they hear the hour,
　Trip through the gloomy courts with haste and
　　fear.

In those high rooms where clients ne'er intrude,
　And here and there a light doth dimly peep,
Each in his lonely set of chambers mewed,
　The briefless crowd their nightly vigils keep.

The grave attorney, knocking frequently,
　The tittering clerk who hastens to the door,

The bulky brief, and corresponding fee,
　　Are things unknown to all that lofty floor.

Small comfort theirs, when each dull day is o'er,
　　No gentle wife their joys and griefs to share,
No quiet homeward walk at half-past four
　　To some snug tenement near Russell Square.

Oft have they read each prosing term report,
　　Dull treatises, and statutes not a few ;
How many a vacant day they've passed in court !
　　How many a barren circuit travell'd through !

Yet let not judges mock their useless toil,
　　And joke at sapient faces no one knows ;
Nor ask, with careless and contemptuous smile,
　　If no one moves in all the long back rows.

Vain is the coif, the ermin'd robe, the strife
　　Of courts, and vain is all success e'er gave ;
Say, can the judge, whose word gives death or life,
　　Reprieve *himself* when summoned to the grave ?

Nor you, ye leaders, view them with ill will,
　　If no one sees their speeches in *The Times*,
Where long-drawn columns oft proclaim your skill
　　To blacken innocence and palliate crimes.

Can legal lore or animated speech
    Avert that sentence which awaits on all?
Can *nisi prius* craft and snares o'erreach
    That Judge, whose look the boldest must appall?

Perhaps in those neglected rooms abound
    Men deeply versed in all the quirks of laws,
Who could, with cases, right and wrong confound,
    And common sense upset by splitting straws.

But ah! to them no clerk his golden page,
    Rich with retaining fees, did e'er unroll;
Chill negligence repressed their legal rage,
    And froze the quibbling current of the soul.

Full many a barrister who well could plead,
    Those dark and unfrequented chambers bear;
Full many a pleader born to draw unfee'd,
    And waste his counts upon the desert air.

Some F—ll—tt, whom no client e'er would trust,
    Some W—lde, who gain'd no verdict in his life;
In den obscure, some D—nm—n there may rust,
    Some C—pb—ll, with no peeress for his wife.

The wits of wondering juries to beguile,
    The wrongs of injured clients to redress,

To gain or lose their verdict with a smile,
  And read their speeches in the daily press,

Their lot forbade.—Nor was it theirs, d'ye see,
  The wretched in the toils of law to lure;
To prostitute their conscience for a fee,
  And shut the gates of justice on the poor.

To try mean tricks to win a paltry cause,
  With threadbare jests to catch the laugh of fools;
Or puff in court, before all human laws,
  The lofty wisdom of the last New Rules.

Not one rule *nisi*, even "to compute,"
  Their gentle voices e'er were heard to pray;
Calm and sequestered, motionless and mute,
  In the remote back seats they passed each day.

Yet e'en their names are sometimes seen in print,
  For frail memorials on the outer doors
Disclose, in letters large and dingy tint,
  The unknown tenants of the upper floors.

Door-posts supply the place of Term Reports,
  And splendid plates around the painter sticks,
To show that he, who never moved the courts,
  Has moved from number two to number six.

For who, to cold neglect a luckless prey,
    His unfrequented attic e'er resigned,
E'er moved with better hopes across the way,
    And did not leave a spruce tin plate behind ?

Strong is the love of fame in noble minds;
    And he whose bold aspirings fate doth crush
Receives some consolation when he finds
    His name recorded by the painter's brush.

For thee, who, mindful of each briefless wight,
    Dost in these motley rhymes their tale relate,
If, musing in his lonely attic flight,
    Some youthful student should inquire thy fate,

Haply some usher of the court may say,—
    "At morn I've mark'd him oft, 'twixt nine and
        ten,
Striding with hasty step the strand away ;
    At four o'clock to saunter back again.

"There in the Bail Court, where yon quaint old
        judge
    Doth twist his nose and wreath his wig awry,—
Listless for hours he'd sit and never budge,
    And pore upon a book—the Lord knows why.

"Oft would he bid me fetch him some report,
  And turn from case to case, with look forlorn;
Then bustling would he run from court to court,
  As if some rule of *his* were coming on.

"One morn I missed that figure lean and lank,
  And that pale face, so often marked by me;
Another came—nor yet was he in Banc,
  Nor th' Exchequer, nor at the Pleas was he.

"The next day, as at morn I chanced to see
  Death's peremptory paper in *The Times,*
I read his name, which there stood number three,
  And there I also read these doleful rhymes:

"EPITAPH.

" Here rests a youth lamented but by few,
  A barrister to fame and courts unknown;
Brief was his life—yet was it briefless too,
  For no attorney marked him for his own.

"Deep and correct his knowledge of the laws,
  No judge a rule of his could e'er refuse;
He never lost a client or a cause,
  Because, forsooth, he ne'er had one to lose.

"E'en as he lived unknown, unknown he dies;
    Calm be his rest, from hopeless struggle free,
Till that dread Court, from which no error lies,
    Shall final judgment pass on him and thee."

THE BRIEF.

As in my chambers, all alone,
  At silent eve I sat,
Indulging a despairing groan,
  I heard a rat-tat-tat;
I started up—I wiped my eye;
  I would not show my grief.
What do I see—what do I spy ?-
  A client with a brief.

I seize it in my eager hand;
  He bids me look within,
That I may shortly understand,
  The cause I fain would win.
I did so—how my lips I bit,
  With rage, despair, and grief!—
There was a copy of a writ
  Folded inside the brief.

THE FIRST CLIENT.

Jᴏʜɴ Sᴍɪᴛʜ, a young attorney, just admitted to the
bar,
Was solemn and sagacious as—as young attorneys
are ;
And a frown of deep abstraction held the seizin of
his face,
The result of contemplation of the rule in Shelley's
Case.

One day in term time Mr. Smith was sitting in the
court,
When some good men and true of the body of the
county did on their oath report,
That heretofore, to wit, upon the second day of
May,
A. D. 1877, about the hour of noon, in the county
and State aforesaid, one Joseph Scroggs, late
of said county, did then and there feloniously
take, steal, and carry away

One bay horse of the value of fifty dollars, more or
less

(The same then and there being of the property,
    goods, and chattels of one Hezekiah Hess),
Contrary to the statute in such case expressly
    made
And provided; and against the peace and dignity
    of the State wherein the venue had been
    laid.

The prisoner, Joseph Scroggs, was then arraigned
    upon this charge,
And plead not guilty, and of this he threw himself
    upon the country at large;
And, said Joseph being poor, the Court did gra-
    ciously appoint
Mr. Smith to defend him —much on the same prin-
    ciple that obtains in every charity hospital
    where a young medical student is often set
    to rectify a serious injury to an organ or a
    joint.

The witnesses seemed prejudiced against poor Mr.
    Scroggs;
And the District Attorney made a thrilling speech,
    in which he told the jury that if they didn't
    find for the State he reckoned he'd have to
    " walk their logs."

Then Mr. Smith arose and made his speech for the
defense,

Wherein he quoted Shakespeare, Blackstone, Chitty,
Archbold, Joaquin Miller, Story, Kent, Tup-
per, Smedes and Marshall, and many other
writers; and everybody said they "never
heered sich a bust of eloquence."

And he said: "On *this* hypothesis, my client must
go free";

And: "Again, on *this* hypothesis, it's morally
impossible that he could be guilty, don't you
see?"

Again: "Then, on *this* hypothesis, you really
can't convict";

And so on, with forty-six more hypotheses, upon
none of which, Mr. Smith ably demonstrated
could Scroggs be derelict.

But the jury, never stirring from the box wherein
they sat,

Returned a verdict of "guilty"; and his Honor
straightway sentenced Scroggs to a three-
year term in the penitentiary, and a heavy
fine, and the costs on top of that;

And the prisoner, in wild delight, got up and danced
    and sung,

And when they asked him the reason of this strange
    behavior, he said: "It's because I got off
    so easy; for, if there'd ha' been a few more
    of them darned *hypothesises*, I should cer-
    tainly have been hung."

15

MONODY ON THE DEATH OF AN ONLY CLIENT.

O TAKE away my wig and gown,
  Their sight is mockery now to me:
I pace my chambers up and down,
  Reiterating, "Where is *he?*"

Alas! wild echo, with a moan,
  Murmurs above my feeble head;
In the wide world I am alone;
  Ha, ha! my only client's dead!

In vain the robing-room I seek,
  The very waiters scarcely bow;
Their looks contemptuously speak,
  "He's lost his only client now."

E'en the mild usher, who of yore
  Would hasten when his name I said
To hand in motions, comes no more;
  He knows my only client's dead.

Ne'er shall I, rising up in court,
  Open the pleadings of a suit;
Ne'er shall the judges cut me short,
  While moving them for a compute.

No more with a consenting brief
 Shall I politely bow my head;
Where shall I run to hide my grief?
 Alas! my only client's dead.

Imagination's magic power
 Brings back, as clear as clear can be,
The spot, the day, the very hour
 When first I signed my maiden plea.

In the exchequer's hindmost row
 I sat, and some one touched my head,
He tendered ten-and-six, but oh!
 That only client now is dead.

In vain I try to sing—I'm hoarse;
 In vain I try to play the flute;
A phantom seems to flit across—
 It is the ghost of a compute.

I try to read, but all in vain;
 My chamber listlessly I tread;
Be still, my heart; throb less, my brain;
 Ho, ho! my only client's dead.

I think I hear a double knock;
 I did—alas! it is a dun.

Tailor, avaunt! my sense you shock;
   He's dead! you know I had but one.

What's this they thrust into my hand?
   A bill returned! ten pounds for bread!
My butcher's got a large demand;
   I'm mad! my only client's dead.

A SUCCESSFUL CAREER.

WHEN a dozen years are over
  Since the ship put out to sea,
Perhaps you may discover
  That you are an A. D.

When eight more years are over,
  And things have got humdrum,
Perhaps you may discover
  That a Sheriff you've become.

When ten more years are over,
  And your faculties need a nudge,
Perhaps you may discover
  That you've been made a Judge.

And when you come to seventy,
  And snow-white is your head,
Perhaps you may discover
  Of a sudden that you're dead.

And when a month is over,
  Since you met the common lot,
Were you living, you'd discover
  That you are quite forgot.

THE VISION AND THE REALITY.

THE VISION.

I'd be a lawyer gifted with power,
    Clients to draw to my little retreat;
I'd pore over Blackstone for many an hour,
    With pleas and rejoinders fill many a sheet;
I'd win every cause, and would eloquence shower,
    Convince judge and jury with arguments meet;
I'd be a lawyer gifted with power,
    Clients to draw to my little retreat.

I ne'er would be drawn from this science away
    By the pleadings of friendship or the soft smile
        of love;
I would study and think for my clients all day,
    And all the delights of fidelity prove.
To fame I would climb, and would toil the steep
        way,
    Nor shrink from the labor if honor approve.
I'd be a lawyer, I'd be a lawyer,
    Nor shrink from the labor if honor approve.

Then say what can equal the advocate's joy
    The oppressor to thwart, the oppressed to defend?

The triumphs of justice have little alloy,
  Fame, honor attending, and wealth in the end.
A name for my country, (how pure is the joy!)
  Untarnished and bright, such a course would
    attend.
I'd be a lawyer, I'd be a lawyer,
  The oppressor to thwart, the oppressed to defend.

THE REALITY.

O, I am a lawyer, and live in a den
  Called an office—a snug and a quiet retreat—
It is sixteen feet one way, the other but ten,
  And the temperature's not far above "fever-heat."
I watch there for clients, but that's all a hum,
Like sprites from the "vasty deep" called—they
  don't come.

I have pen, paper, ink, and blank writs a good
    store,
  Three chairs, and a table, a day-book, and docket;
Get five writs a term, a defense or two more,
  Am *plus* in my idleness, *minus* in pocket;
To persuade court and jury I argue all day,
And convince them it's right to decide t'other way.

So much for the profit and pleasure.   And now,
  The account as to honor pray let us be casting;

That there's fame to be had, I most freely allow:
  People "damn" the profession "to fame ever-
    lasting";
They'll tell you a lawyer but seeks for the pelf,
And for that will out-Herod the D——l himself.

A WHIMSICAL ATTORNEY'S BILL.

A BILL OF CHARGES, JUSTLY DUE,

FROM A. B. C. TO S. T. U.

	£	s.	d.
ATTENDING for instructions, when			
Your honor bade me call again,	0	6	8
The like attendance, time the second,			
Which as before is fairly reckoned,	0	6	8
Taking instructions given to me			
For drawing up your pedigree,	0	6	8
Perusing said instructions to			
Consider whether right or no,	0	6	8
You form the scale in just perfection,			
I therefore only charge inspection,	0	6	8
Drawing up pedigree complete,			
Fair copy (closely wrote), one sheet,	0	6	8
Attending to examine same,			
And adding Tom to William Naim,	0	6	8
Addendum of Sir Darcy's birth,	0	6	8
Paid Porter's coach hire, and so forth,	0	5	6
Fair copy of this bill of cost,	0	2	0
Another, for the first was lost,	0	2	0
Advice, time, trouble, and my care			
In settling this perplexed affair,	1	1	0

Writing receipt at foot of bill,	0	3	4
My clerk—but give him what you will,	0	0	0
	4	7	2

Received of A. B. C. aforesaid
The full contents: what can be more said?

S. T. U.

THE BACHELOR'S DREAM.

A' NICHT I'm haunted by a shape,
In weeds o' dool and bran-new crape,
A fillet reid o' office-tape,
    Medusan locks in 'mid o';
I ken her weel, although she haud
Her ill-faure'd face intil her maud,
It's that—it's that contingent jaud,
    My widow.

Ilk towmont in the month o' June,
I get Hall-marked like ony spune,
And five gude punds, a croon abune,
    I bude to mak' me rid o',
That's a' for her; sae though I crane
Roond by her haffits a' in vain,
It's her, or I am sair mista'en,
    My widow.

" I'm tell't," wi' gruesome tane quo' she,
" Twa coontin chiels a Committeé,
And aiblins mair wi' thocht o' me,
    Are unco mystified, O

Lat them collogue, be't wrang or richt,
But min my Jo, I rede ye ticht
Ye'll rue the day ye daured to slicht
  Your widow."

Says ane, "I fegs I'll pay nae mair,
The pickle gowd I ill can spare,
For hags that leeve far yont their share,
  Like them bafore the Flude, O,
Gudeman the chiel his wits has tint.
I daur ye to sae much as mint,
For twa three motion-fees, to stint
  Your widow."

Anither says: "The bits o' weans,
No auld eneuch to fend their lanes,
They maun ha'e duds to cuire their banes,
  And warm their orphan blude, O.
Na, na, let Heriot's cleed the brats,
And stairve or kill them wi' the bats,
There's ane comes *primo loco* that's—
  Your widow."

"I'll marry ye to please mysell,
I'll gie ye some sma taste o' ——,
And syne I'll kist ye in your shell,
  And blithely steek the lid, O.

Than gin ye le'e me bune the grund,
Wi' nocht o' tocher but the Fund,
Wha'll pree wi' sax and saxty pund,
     Your widow?"

Sae ilka nicht she'll crack and glowre,
Frae midnicht to the chap o' foure,
I sweat and swarf, and ower and ower
     I wuss her at Megiddo.
I'm dwinin' fast, I'm well nigh spent,
I'll vote to raise the annual rent,
I'll vote for aucht that will content,
     My widow.

16

MY WIDOW.

A BACHELOR born (a common fate),
And doomed to die a celibate,
Still I must pay thine annual rate,
   My widow!

I'm trapped! A wife you may divorce,
Get rid of her by fraud or force;
With thee there's no such blest resource,
   My widow!

No wife in this drear world have I;
And in the other, when I die,
Thy sweet face will not greet my eye,
   My widow!

Mateless in both worlds thus I am;
Yet I *must* pay, O shameful sham!
No wonder that I often damn
   My widow!

Doubly bereft, 'tis I should be
Put on the Fund ; and yet on.thee
Devolves the snug annuity,
   My widow!

Full many a maid have I embraced;
But never did I clasp thy waist,
Nor nectar of thy lips did taste,
My widow!

What art thou like? Art dark or fair?
With carroty or raven hair?
Of common or *distingué* air?
My widow!

" With meek and unaffected grace,"
Dost thou put on a pious face?
Dost *girn* or giggle or grimace?
My widow!

"You pay your money, take your choice,"
In all things else; but I've no voice
In that which does they heart rejoice,
My widow!

Ah! never shall I call thee wife;
Ne'er see thy lineaments in life;
Never enjoy connubial strife,
My widow!

From death's dim realm a ghostly hand
I'll stretch to thee and all the band
Of shadowy babes that round thee stand,
My widow!

We ne'er shall see (at which I'm grieved)
Our family, all unachieved;
Conceivable, but unconceived,
   My widow!

MONBODDO.

THE thought that men had once had tails
  Caused many a grin full broad, O;
And why in us that feature fails,
  Was asked of old Monboddo.
He showed that sitting on the rump,
  While at our work we plod, O,
Would wear the appendage to the stump,
  As close as in Monboddo.

Alas! the good lord little knew,
  As this strange ground he trod, O,
That others would his path pursue,
  And never name Monboddo!
Such folks should have their tails restored,
  And thereon feel the rod, O,
For having thus the fame ignored
  That's due to old Monboddo.

Though Darwin now proclaim the law,
  And spread it far abroad, O,
The man that first the secret saw,
  Was honest old Monboddo.

THE PROCESS OF WAKENING.

AIR—"Peggie is over ye Sie wi' ye Souldier."—*Skene MS.*

JENNY! puir Jenny! the flow'r o' the lea—
The blithesome, the winsome, the gentle an' free—
    The joy and the pride
    O' the kintra side—
She dee'd of a process o' wakening.

Though her skin was sae smooth an' her fingers sae
    sma',
She won through the whoopin'-cough, measles,
    an' a'—
    She never took ill
    Frae fever or chill—
Yet she dee'd of a process o' wakening.

The case fell asleep when her grandfather dee'd;
And few folk remembered it e'er had been plea'd.
    She never heard tell
    O' the matter hersel',
Till they sent her the summons o' wakening.

Jenny! puir Jenny!—though courted by a',
Only ane touched her heart—an' he bore it awa.

It had just been arranged
That her state should be changed,
When they sent her the summons o' wakening.

She had plighted her troth; they had fixed on the
    day;
A' arrangements completed—nae chance o' delay;
    She was thinkin' on this,
    And entrancéd wi' bliss,
When they sent her the summons o' wakening.

Her friends were sae kindly, her true-love sae
    prized;
Surrounded by them, an' by him idolized;
    She had just passed the night
    In a dream o' delight,
When they sent her the summons o' wakening.

She fee'd the best counsel—what could she do mair?
She read through the papers wi' sorrow an' care,
    But could only mak out,
    That beyond ony doubt,
'Twas a wearifu' process o' wakening.

An' her friends that she thought wad be constant
    for aye,
Of course they grew scarce, an' kept out o' her way;

For naebody ken'd
How the matter wad end,
When they heard o' the process o' wakening.

An' her true-love, for whom she wad gladly gien a',
Slid cauld frae her grasp, like a bullet o' snaw ;—
Sae she gied up the case,
An' gied up the ghaist,
An' dee'd o' a process o' wakening.

SOUMIN AND ROUMIN.

"Where divers heritors have a common pasturage in one commonty, no part whereof is ever plowed, the said common pasturage may be *soumed* and *roumed*, that all the *soums* the whole commonty can hold may be determined and proportioned to each *roum* having the common pasturage, according to the holding of that *roum*."—*Case of the Laird of Drumalzier, Stair's Decisions*, ii. 678.

Air—"Hooly and Fairly."

My Grannie!—she was a worthy auld woman;
She keepit three geese an' a cow on a common.
Puir body!—she sune made her fu' purse a toom ane,
By raisin' a process o' Soumin and Roumin.
                    Soumin and Roumin—
                By raising a process o'
                    Soumin and Roumin.

A young writer lad put it into her head;
He gi'ed himsel' out for a dab at the trade—
For guidin' a plea or a proof quite uncommon,
And a terrible fellow at Soumin and Roumin.
                    Soumin and Roumin, etc.

He took her three geese to get it begun,
And he needit her cow to carry it on,

Syne she gi'ed him her band for the cost that was
    comin',
And on went the process o' Soumin and Roumin.
                  Soumin and Roumin, etc.

My Grannie she grieved, and my grannie she graned,
As she paid awa ilk honest groat she had hained;
She sat in her elbow-chair, glow'rin' and gloomin',
Speakin' o' naething but Soumin and Roumin.
                  Soumin and Roumin, etc.

She caredna for meat, and she caredna for drink;
By night or by day she could ne'er sleep a wink.
" O Lord, pity me, for a wicked auld woman!
It's a sair dispensation, this Soumin and Roumin."
                  Soumin and Roumin, etc.

In vain did the writer lad promise success—
Speak of Interim Decrees and final redress;
In vain did he tell her that judgment was comin'—
"It's a judgment already, this Soumin and Roumin!"
                  Soumin and Roumin, etc.

The doctor was sent for—but what could he say?
He allowed the complaint to be out o' his way;
The priest spak' o' Job—said to suffer was human;
But she said, "Job kent naething o' Soumin and
    Roumin."
                  Soumin and Roumin, etc.

The priest tried to pray, and the priest tried to read,
But she wadna attend to ae word that he said;
She made a bad end for sae guid an auld woman—
Her death-rattle sounded like "Soumin and Rou-
min."
Soumin and Roumin, etc.

I'm executor—heir-male—o' line—an' provision—
An' the writer lad says that he'll manage the seisin;
But of a' the estate, there's naething forthcomin',
But a guid-gangin' process o' Soumin and Roumin.
Soumin and Roumin, etc.

BALLADS OF THE BRIEFLESS.

THE RULE TO COMPUTE.

O, TELL me not of empires grand,
    Of proud dominion wide and far,
Of those who sway the fertile land
    Where melons three for twopence are.
To rule like this I ne'er aspire ;
    In fact, my book it would not suit!
The only *rule* that I desire,
    Is *a rule nisi to compute.*

O, speak not of the calm delights,
    That in the fields or lanes we win;
The field and lane that me invites
    Is Chancery or Lincoln's Inn.
Yes, there in some remote recess
    At eve, I practice on my flute,
Till some attorney comes to bless
    With *a rule nisi to compute.*

SIGNING A PLEA.

O, now oft when alone at the close of the day
    I've sat in that Court where the fig-tree don't grow,

And wonder'd how I, without money, should pay
   The little account to my laundress below!
And when I have heard a quick step on the stair,
   I've thought which of twenty rich duns it could
     be,
I have rushed to the door in a fit of despair,
   And—*received ten and sixpence for signing a plea.*

Chorus.—Signing a plea, signing a plea!
      Received ten and sixpence for signing a
      plea.

They may talk as they will of the pleasure that's
     found,
   When venting in verse our despondence and grief;
But the pen of the poet was ne'er, I'll be bound,
   Half so pleasantly used as in signing a brief.
In soft declarations, though rapture may lie,
   If the maid to appear to your suit willing be.
But ah! I could write till my inkstand was dry,
   And die in the act—yes—of signing a plea.

Chorus.—Signing a plea, signing a plea!
      Die in the act—yes—of signing a plea.

17

A MISJOINDER.

O THAT some genius would write a report
Of the things that are done in this dignified Court,
Where pigs, men, and horses, and other lean cattle
With their lawyers all drawn up in order of battle,
Are gathered together in great agitation,
To end their contention in fierce litigation!
First, cometh Judge Robbins, in debt and in trover
A misjoinder in pleading too bad to pass over;
But, after demurring and wrangling like fury,
The Court took the pleadings—the counsel a jury.
The witnesses came, and proved that one Hanks
Had lately been guilty of barbarous pranks,
In this, that without conscience or twinge of remorse,
He took up a gentleman's city-bred horse,
And put him to plowing like any old hack;
He "cussed" him, he flogged him, made sores on his
      back;
He starved him so badly, "inverted the blessings,"
And gave the old horse such a number of dressings,
That when Mr. Taylor, the lawyer, had found him,
The bugs and the buzzards had gathered around him.
The evidence through—the lawyers are pitted,
The speeches are made, and the case is submitted—

The jury retire—the verdict soon follows,
That Hanks shall pay Robbins full twenty round
      dollars ;
But the Court, in the pleadings detecting a flaw,
Administers *Justice* according to *law*,
By ordering these litigant sons of Belial
To mend up their pleadings and take a new trial.

THE ORDERLY PARTS OF PLEADING.

A DECLARATION on the plaintiff's part
Is first in course, with this the pleadings start.
The next in order comes defendant's *plea ;*
Should plaintiff to the *plea* reply, 'twill be
His *replication*, as you'll plainly see.
Rejoinder follows, if defendant *plead,*
The plaintiff's *sur rejoinder* then may lead,
Rebutter still defendant may insist ;
The *sur rebutter* closes up the list.
No further pleas on either side are brought.
The *ne plus ultra* has been found not sought.
Just seven links make up this legal chain ;
The last link reached, to seek for more were vain.
The real *issue* must be somewhere found,
To which contending parties may be bound !
This *issue* must be one of *law* or *fact ;*
It must be single, this the rules exact,
Also *certain* and *material*, too—
For if upon a clear and fair review
The requisites are not all clearly found,
The *issue* reached will be declared unsound.
These brief and simple rules here introduced
Will tend to show how issues are produced.

The first is this: that after plaintiff's *plea*,
Or *declaration*, it should rather be,
The parties must at each successive stage
Demur or *plead*, and thus their battle wage
By way of *traverse*, or they may instead
In confession and avoidance plead.
The substance of rule second seems to be,
That when a *traverse* is a party's plea,
Issue must be tendered then and there;
The rule's imperative and plainly fair.
Lastly: an *issue* tendered well must be
Accepted.   The law permits no further plea.
Were this not so, the matter in dispute
Could not appear, and bootless then the suit;
Juries would be a farce, and courts a form,
And pleading of its only province shorn.
Pleading is based on logic, that is clear;
And he the best logician will appear
Who can for all its many rules supply
A reason, or, in other words, the why.
For earnest students there's a royal road
To legal lore, which leads *beyond* the " code,"
Stretching far on to where a temple stands,
Whose towering heights the law's broad field com-
        mands.
This stately temple, reached in ages past,
Is firm, compact, and of proportions vast.

By slow degrees the massive structure grew;
Its workmen wrought with vigor ever new;
Age follows age, and still the work goes on;
Art, learning, genius, all their stores were drawn,
And yet this monument to legal lore,
To LAW and LAWYERS sacred evermore,
Stood forth complete; 'tis now the scholar's pride,
The law's delight, the pleader's *only* guide.
But I digress, digression here must end,
Or leave will not be granted to *amend;*
Nor yet be *aided* after verdict given;
So then right here I'll ask to be forgiven,
Or plead to all not strictly *legal* matter,
Utile per inutile non vitiatur.

JURY TRIAL IN THE DAYS OF EDWARD I.

'Tis forty pennies that you ask, a ransom fine for
    me;
And twenty more, 'tis but a score, for my lord sher-
    iff's fee:
Else of his deepest dungeon the darkness I must
    dree;
Is this of justice, masters?—Behold my case and
    see.

For this I'll to the greenwood—to the pleasant
    shade away;
There evil none of law doth wonne, nor harmful
    perjury.
I'll to the wood, the pleasant wood, where freely
    flies the jay;
And, without fail, the nightingale is chanting of
    her lay.

But for that cursed *dozen*, God show them small
    pitie;
Among their lying voices they have indicted me,
Of wicked robberies and other felonie,
That I dare no more, as heretofore, among my
    friends to be.

In peace and war my service my Lord, the King,
    hath ta'en,
In Flanders and in Scotland, and Gascoyne his
    domain;
But now I'll never, well I wis, be mounted man
    again,
To pleasure such a man as this I've spent much
    time in vain.

But if these cursed *jurors* do not amend them so,
That I to my own country may freely ride and go,
The head that I can come at shall jump when I've
    my blow,
Their menacings, and all such things, then to the
    winds I'll throw.

All ye who are indicted, I pray you come to me,
To the greenwood, the pleasant wood, where's nei-
    ther suit nor plea;
But only the wild creatures, and many a spreading
    tree;
For there's little in the common law but doubt and
    misery.

If meeting a companion, I show my archery,
My neighbor will be saying, "He's of some com-
    pany—

He goes to cage him in the wood, and worke his
    old foleye ";
For men will hunt me like the boar, and life's no
    life for me.

If I should seem more cunning about the law than
    they,
"Ha! ha! some old conspirator, well trained in
    tricks," they'll say;
O wheresoe'er doth ride the Eyre, I must keep
    well away :—
Such neighborhood I hold not good, shame fall on
    such I pray.

I pray you all, good people, to say for me a prayer,
That I in peace may once again to my own land
    repair:
I never was a homicide, not with my will, I swear,
Nor robber, Christian folk to spoil, that on their
    way did fare.

This rhyme was made within the wood, beneath a
    broad bay-tree;
There singeth merle and nightingale, and falcon
    soareth free.
I wrote the skin, because within was much sore
    memory,
And here I fling it by the wood, that found my
    rhyme may be.

THE PET OF THE BRITISH JURY.

To Trial by Jury Britons owe
 The happiness of being free;
'Tis called, because the fact is so,
 Palladium of our liberty.
A jury is the wisest plan,
 Whenever folks each other sue,
That ever was devised by man
 For rendering unto all their due.

A British Jury knows no fear,
 No favour does it e'er display
To Rank and Wealth, to Prince or Peer,
 Who try twelve upright souls to sway;
Impartial both to rich and poor,
 To neither class disposed to bend,
The British Jury evermore
 Is found the British Tradesman's friend.

When for his bill—however large—
 An action he's compelled to bring,
If British Jurors dock his charge,
 O, how extremely rare a thing!
From an expensive minor's sire,
 Or an indebted lady's mate,

Of any sum he may require,
  How seldom will they aught abate!

Should any aged trifler break
  His infant daughter's tender heart
By breach of promise—don't they make
  The toothless old deceiver smart!
The Juryman and Father feels
  The Tradesman's and the Father's pain,
The British Tradesman ne'er appeals
  To British Jurymen in vain.

The other day a case occurred,
  Whereof the justice all must own,
The *Times* contained a tale absurd,
  How that a tailor—name unknown–
An army-clothier's agent—not
  Denoted even by a dash,
Had out in the Crimea got
  Scored by the Provost-Marshal's lash.

Although this story was a myth,
  To common vision very dim,
There was a certain tailor, Smith,
  And his friends fixed it upon him;
An action 'gainst the *Times* he brought
  Upon these solid serious grounds,

A British Jury gave him naught
 Less than just full four hundred pounds.

Nine injured British Tailors, they
 Did, sure, in that one Tradesman see,
And so condemned the *Times* to pay
 For damage done to three times three;
Then sing, Nine tailors make a man,
 And in a box there were twelve geese;
So of four hundred pounds we can
 Make forty-four pounds odd apiece.

A DIGEST OF LORD —— 'S EVIDENCE

BEFORE THE ROYAL COMMISSION AS TO JURY TRIALS.

I.

It may be dramatic, it doubtless is dear;
  But yet I most strongly assure ye,
To assess what's to pay, to turn dark into clear,
  There's nothing like trial by jury.

II.

A Judge may go wrong, I frequently do,
  Both in questions of law and of fact;
The counsel look black, and the agents look blue,
  But I hide my annoyance with tact.

III.

When the Court overturns what on proof I have
      found,
  And the litigants get in a fury,
It only *confirms* the view I prŏpound,
  That the case should have gone to a jury.

18

LIGHT FROM AN EMINENT S. S. C.

"Ex noto fictum Carmen sequar."—Hor

A TRIAL by jury I always have felt,
　Might be done in a different way ;
But counsel are flurried and agents are hurried
　Through provincial employer's delay.

Yet the evils are few, in fact, they are two,
　Where trial by jury is wrong :
There are witnesses brought, whether needed or not,
　And the evidence led is too long.

To decrease this expense, which I think is immense,
　In a trial by jury or proof,
I will mention a way the expense to defray,
　Which is certainly free from reproof.

To the counsel I say, "See these witnesses, they
　Are bad, or superfluous, chiefly ;
But we'll lose the expense and give them offense,
　Unless you examine them briefly."

In the last of my proofs two counsel I fee'd,
　As I thought, if I only had one,
He might not attend, but alas ! in the end
　I found myself sitting alone.

The plan I suggest, when the motions are called,
  Such an evil as this to reform
(For I seldom as yet any counsel could get
  Who had leisure his work to perform),

Is to hold that the Judge, by a *fictio juris*,
  To chambers has suddenly fled;
And if counsel's not there, let the agent prepare,
  Or his clerk, to address him instead.

When an agent is paid for his work, it is said
  His client expects him to do it;
And I always have thought that the bar might be got
  To act on this rule, if they knew it.

But I do not intend that a counsel should send
  His clerk to conduct a debate,
And pocket the fee — to such cases, you see,
  The rule is not meant to relate.

In the case of a fee, it is plain as can be,
  That the maxim of law so well known,
Qui facit per alium facit per se,
  Is intended for agents alone.

On the part of "our body" I wish to allow,
  Since employment we give to so few,
More intelligent counsel, more able than now,
  We think that the bar never knew.

THE JURY-LAW VICTIM.

DEDICATED TO THE ATTORNEY-GENERAL.

Summoned to serve on a jury!
  O, I shall go to the bad!
Driven with distraction and fury,
  Ruin in prospect, stark mad.
Dragged from the work that's my living,
  Other men's business to mind,
I shall no thought have for giving
  Save to my own, left behind.

Truly to try they may swear me,
  Off mine employment when torn;
Whilst my anxieties tear me,
  What can I be but forsworn?
Counsel will vainly harangue me,
  Witness depose all in vain,
Judge's charge—though he could hang me—
  Naught of my mind will obtain.

As for all criminal cases,
  I shall the prisoner acquit,
Like a deaf man's while my place is;
  Give him the doubt's benefit.

And in all civil, as hearing
   Not either side what they say,
I shall toss up, that appearing
   Nearest for me the right way.

If you'd have juries' attention
   Pay your confounded affairs,
Press men by fortune, or pension,
   Freed from life's personal cares,
Idle is all adjuration
   When the adjured are not free.
So much for the administration
   Of justice you'll get out of me!

JUROR NUMBER SIX.

And so you wonder, do you, why the jury disagreed
　In that case of Thompson, tried at August court,
For stealing Jones's mare — the one of thorough
　　breed—
　　That took the eyes of all, and made them hanker
　　　for it.

Well, I'll tell you how it was, for I was on the
　　panel,
　Being number six as was called out by the clerk,
And I thought, as in the box I went, that man'll
　　Find that justice hunts out crime, however dark.

Half a day they speeched and witnessed on the sub-
　　ject,
　Proof was thin, I vow, but talk was over-thick,
And old Thompson sat there, brazen-faced, in pub-
　　lic,
　With a look of innocence that made me almost
　　sick.

Then for consultation out did march the jury,
　And eleven of them straightway did decide

Thompson is "not guilty," and broke out in a fury
　When with such a view I said I couldn't coin-
　　cide.

But they were very stubborn, though I tried each
　　man, sir,
　To convince him of his error—so you see,
When the court again met for our answer
　We had none to give but that "we disagree."

And now I'll tell you further—keep it very quiet—
　Thompson was not guilty, that is fair and square,
For, you see, as being rather poor to buy it,
　Juror Number Six, it was, sir, stole old Jones's
　　mare.

SONGS OF THE CIRCUIT.

THE HOME.

From Circuit to Circuit although we may roam,
Be it ever so briefless, there's none like the Home;
A fee from the skies p'rhaps may follow us there,
Which, seek through the Courts, is ne'er met with
      elsewhere.
Home, Home, sweet sweet Home,
There's none of the Circuits can equal the Home.

When out on the Home, lodgings tempt you in vain,
The railroad brings you back to your chambers
      again;
On the Home the expenses for posting are small;
Give me that—'tis the Circuit, the cheapest of all.
Home, Home, sweet, sweet Home,
There's none of the Circuits can equal the Home.

THE MISSISSIPPI WITNESS.

Yoah Honah, an' de Jury: Ef you'll listen, now,
    to me,
I's gwine to straighten up dis case jes like it ought
    to be;
Dis heah's a case ob stealing' hogs—a mighty ser'ous
    'fense—
An' you'll know all about it, when I gibs my ebby-
    dence.

Dis Peter Jones, de plainter, is a member ob de
    chuc'h,
But Thomas Green, de fender, goodness knows he's
    nuffin much—
A lazy, triflin' nigger is dat berry Thomas Green—
Dese is de dif'rent parties you is called to jedge
    atween

Now, gib me stric' contention while I 'lucidates de
    fac':
Dere's two whole sides to eberyting—de front one
    au' de back.
What's dat de little lawyer say? To talk about de
    case?
Dat's jus what I wuz comin' to; you makes me lose
    de place.

Whar wuz I? O, I 'members; I wuz jes about to
    say,
I heerd a disputation 'bout a p'int of law, to-
    day—
Bout how to turn State's ebbydence—dat's what
    dey's dribin' at—
Now ain't it strange some niggers is so ignorant as
    dat?

Why, when you wants to turn it, you jes has to
    come to town,
An' fin' de Deestric Turner—he'll be somewhar
    loafin' 'roun'—
An' den sez you, "Mahs Turner, sah, I zires my
    compliments;
I's come in town to see you, for to turn State's eb-
    bydence."

As soon's you tells him dat, he knows perzackly
    what you mean,
An' takes you to his office, where he's got a big
    mersheen,
An' dar you catches hol' de crank, an' den you turns
    away,
Untell at las' dar's somefin' clicks, an' den you's come
    to A.

" Is dat de letter ob de thing de feller done?" says
  he ;
Ef you says no, you turns agin untell you comes to B;
An' so you keeps a-turnin', tell de right one gits
  aroun',
An' dar de Deestric Turner looks, an' dar de law
  is foun'.

An' den you gibs de fac's, an' den he reads de law
  to you,
An' axes you to 'vise him what you think he ought
  to do;
An' den he say, " Good mornin'," an' he gibs you
  fifty cents,
An' dat's de way you has to do to turn State's ebbydence.

Well, gemmen of de jury, dis heah case is under-
  stood,
I doesn't *know* de hog wuz stole, but Peter's word
  is good—
He up an' sesso manfully, dout makin' any bones ;
An' darfore, sahs, if I wuz you, I think I'd 'cide for
  Jones.

THE DEMISE OF DOE AND ROE.

(Obierunt July 15, 1852.)

In Westminster Hall it is darkness all,
And solemn the strokes of midnight fall
 From out the neighboring Abbey tower ;
The echoes call, from roof and wall,
 And pass the record of the hour.

The first has died, the last replied,
That 'twixt the far roof ribs doth hide,
 And midnight hath been signalled round,
When the Court doors wide, on the western side,
 Fly open all, without a sound.

From each doth troop a shadowy group
Of forms that 'neath a burden stoop—
 A heavy burden like a bier ;
Mournfully their heads they droop,
 Their sobs and sighs are plain to hear.

Doleful and drear about the bier,
Whereon two shrouded forms appear,
 Laid out like corpses, side by side:
No corpses, though, for lo ! they rear
 Two grizzly heads, all hollow-eyed !

Heavy as lead, from each bier-bed,
Is lifted up a stricken head.
　　But hold! methinks those heads I know—
Law-bred, law-fed, but now nigh sped—
　　It is JOHN DOE and RICHARD ROE!

Well I know them; naught I owe them;
Oft, in an ejectment (blow them!),
　　ROE I have cursed and DOE have demmed;
Law that made doth now o'erthrow them,
　　And now to die they are condemned.

Now, erecter, grisley spectre,
ROE, the casual ejector,
　　Sadly sits up and strives to speak;
DOE, that once stormed like a HECTOR,
　　Bears to his comrade burden meek:

"Legal fictions, our afflictions
Should to you be as predictions
　　To tell your quickly coming fate;
New reforms and fresh restrictions
　　Are gathering all about law's gate.

"Ye are many, yet not any
Brought the lawyers such a penny
　　As we great fictions used to do;
19

Never cats of famed Kilkenny
   Such battles fought as did we two.

"The great glory of our story,
On the page of year-books hoary,
   In old black-letter may be read;
Gallant were our fights and gory,
   For in the purse our victims bled.

"In the nation's declarations
We have ruled for generations;
   Still at our will, unjust or just,
We flung the proud from their high stations,
   We raised the lowly from their dust.

"Although we were not things, but names,
All in our keeping left their claims,
   Inspired with reverent awe.
Deaf to men's praises or their blames,
   We sat—lies throned on law.

"Till the bold ways of these new days
Dared question of our use to raise,
   And insolently sought to know
If justice *must* walk in a maze,
   Led by the ghosts of Doe and Roe?

"Still bolder grew the impious crew,
And more and more the veil withdrew
   That hangs before the shrine of law;
And though we stood revealed to view,
   Stoutly declared they nothing saw.

"Reckless they swore they would no more
Be dupes of fictions, as of yore;
   And on this frivolous pretence,
Into the cave of legal lore
   Let the coarse light of common sense.

"Our sand is run—our reign is done,
The accursed light we may not shun,
   We sink beneath its fatal ray;
You, minor fictions, every one,
   Before it soon must melt away.

"With Doe and me soon men will see
Poor formal color in a plea;
   And you, ye Common Courts, also;
You, forms of action, soon will be,
   Where Doe and I are going to.

"Rules to Compute, you'll soon be mute—
Special demurrers, keen and 'cute,
   Your quibbles will not save you long;

You, too, Venires, branch and root,
    Will fall before the reckless throng.

" In this last hour, with prophet power,
I see as one sees from a tower,
    Law, shorn and shaved, and short,
Driven from her ancient state, to lower
    In cheap and nasty County Court.

"Gone pleaders' sleight to prove wrong right;
Gone subtle forms to make black white;
    Gone every quibble, quiddit, quirk,
All that make suitors' purses light,
    And all that found the lawyers work.

" To end doth draw the reign of Law;
Merits shall win, despite of flaw,
    Whether in process or in plea—
Justice comes in, rude, coarse, and raw,
    And so, friends, out go we!"

THE CIRCUITEER'S LAMENT.

AE morning near the dawning, I saw a counsel
yawning,
And heard him say in accents that were onything
but gay,
As sadly he was grinding at a meikle multiplepoin-
ding ;
The days o' my Circuits are a' fled away.

Nae processions, nae pageants, nae pawky country
agents,
Nae macers, nae trumpeters, wi' tipsy blare and
bray,
Nae councillor or bailie, or provost smiling gayly ;
The days o' my Circuits are a' fled away.

Nae funny cross-examining, nae jurymen begam-
moning,
Nae laughter from the audience, nae gallery's
hurrah,
Nae fleeching for acquittal, though you don't care
a spittle ;
The days o' my Circuits are a' fled away.

Nae playing hocus-pocus with the *tempus* and the
    locus,
  Nae pleas in mitigation (a kittle job are they),
Nae bonny rapes and reivings, nae forgeries and
    thievings;
  The days o' my Circuits are a' fled away.

Nae banter frae Lord D——s, nae promises of fees
  That never will be paid afore the Judgment Day,
Nae lies dubbed "information," from the warst
    rogues in the nation;
  The days o' my Circuits are a' fled away.

Nae haveral "wutty" witness displaying his unfit-
    ness
  To see some sma' distinction 'tween a trial and a
    play;
Nae witness primed at lunch wi' perjuries and punch;
  The days o' my Circuits are a' fled away.

Nae laughing-gas orations, nae treading on the
    patience
  Of judges and of juries, who let you say your say,
Yet pay but sma' attention to the gems of your in-
    vention;
  The days o' my Circuits are a' fled away.

Nae mair delightful wond₍ring, at a new man bland-
ly blundering,
Nae kind hints from the Court that he's ganging
far astray;
Nae flowery depictions, in the teeth of ten convic-
tions,
The days o' my Circuits are a' fled away.

Nae whacking ten years' sentence, wi' advices to
repentance,
And learn in years of leisure to admire " the
law's delay,"
Nae fell female fury, blackguarding judge and jury;
The days o' my Circuits are a' fled away.

Nae grey auld woman sobbing, nae mair ye'll catch
her robbing,
And a' the Christian virtues henceforth she will
display,
If the judge will but have mercy (for the sixteenth
time I dare say) ;
The days o' my Circuits are a' fled away.

Nae dinners with the judges, nae drooning a' your
grudges,
In deep, deep draughts of claret, and a' your
senses tae;

Nae chatter wise or witty on ticklish points of
    dittay ;
The days o' my Circuits are a' fled away.

Nae high jinks after dinner wi' ony madcap sinner,
    Nae drinking whisky toddy, until the break of
    day,
Nae speeches till a hiccup compels a sudden stick-up ;
The nichts o' my Circuits are a' fled away.

A CASE OF LIBEL.

"The greater the truth, the worse the libel."

A CERTAIN sprite, who dwells below,
 ('Twere a libel, perhaps, to mention where,)
Came up, *incog.*, some years ago,
 To try, for a change, the London air.

So well he look'd and dress'd and talk'd,
 And hid his tail and horns so handy,
You'd hardly have known him, as he walk'd,
 From C***e or any other dandy.

(His horns, it seems, are made t' unscrew ;
 So he has but to take them out of the socket,
And—just as some fine husbands do—
 Conveniently clap them into his pocket.)

In short, he look'd extremely natty,
 And ev'n contriv'd—to his own great wonder—
By dint of sundry scents from Gattie,
 To keep the sulphurous *hogo* under.

And so my gentleman hoof'd about,
 Unknown to all but a chosen few,
At White's and Crockford's, where, no doubt,
 He had many *post obits* falling due.

Alike a gamester and a wit,
 At night he was seen with Crockford's crew,
At morn with learned dames would sit,
 So pass'd his time 'twixt *black* and *blue*.

Some wished to make him an M P.,
 But finding Wilks was also one, he
Swore, in a rage, he'd be d——d if he
 Would ever sit in one house with Johnny.

At length, as secrets travel fast,
 And devils, whether he or she,
Are sure to be found out at last,
 The affair got wind most rapidly.

The Press, the impartial Press, that snubs
 Alike a fiend's or an angel's capers—
Miss Paton's soon as Beelzebub's—
 Fired off a squib in the morning papers:

" We warn good men to keep aloof
 From a grim old dandy seen about,
With a fire-proof wig, and a cloven hoof
 Through a neat-cut Hoby smoking out."

Now, the Devil being a gentleman,
 Who piques himself on well-bred dealings,

You may guess, when o'er these lines he ran,
  How much they hurt and shock'd his feelings.

Away he posts to a man of law,
  And O, 'twould make you laugh to 've seen 'em.
As paw shook hand, and hand shook paw,
  And 'twas "hail, good fellow, well met," between
    'em.

Straight an indictment was preferr'd,
  And much the Devil enjoy'd the jest,
When, asking about the Bench, he heard
  That of all the Judges his own was *Best*.1

In vain defendant proffer'd proof,
  That plaintiff's self was the Father of Evil,
Brought Hoby forth, to swear to the hoof,
  And Stultz to speak to the tail of the Devil.

The jury (saints all snug and rich,
  And readers of virtuous Sunday papers)
Found for the plaintiff—on hearing which
  The Devil gave one of his loftiest capers.

For O, 'twas nuts to the Father of Lies
  (As this wily fiend is named in the Bible),
To find it settled, by laws so wise,
  That the greater the truth, the worse the libel!

REPORT OF AN ADJUDGED CASE,

NOT TO BE FOUND IN ANY OF THE BOOKS.

BETWEEN Nose and Eyes a strange contest arose,
  The spectacles set them unhappily wrong;
The point in dispute was, as all the world knows,
  To which the said spectacles ought to belong.

So Tongue was the lawyer, and argued the cause
  With a great deal of skill, and a wig full of learn-
    ing;
While Chief Baron Ear sat to balance the laws,
  So famed for his talent of nicely discerning.

In behalf of the Nose, it will quickly appear,
  And your lordship, he said, will undoubtedly find,
That the nose has had spectacles always in wear,
  Which amounts to possession time out of mind.

Then holding the spectacles up to the Court,
  Your lordship observes they are made with a
    straddle
As wide as the bridge of the nose is; in short,
  Designed to sit close to it, just like a saddle.

Again: would your lordship a moment suppose
  ('Tis a case that has happen'd, and may be again)
That the visage or countenance had not a Nose,
    Pray who would, or who could, wear spectacles
      then?

On the whole, it appears, and my argument shows,
  With a reasoning the Court will never condemn,
That the spectacles plainly were made for the Nose,
  And the Nose was as plainly intended for them.

Then shifting his side (as a lawyer knows how),
  He pleaded again in behalf of the Eyes;
But what were his arguments few people know,
  For the Court did not think they were equally wise.

So his lordship decreed, with a grave, solemn tone,
  Decisive and clear, without one if or but,
That whenever the Nose put his spectacles on,
  By daylight or candle-light, Eyes must be shut!

20

HAT *VS.* WIG.

" Metus omnes et inexorabile fatum
Subjecit pedibus, strepitumque Acheroutis avari."

'Twixt Eldon's Hat and Eldon's Wig
  There lately rose an altercation,
Each with its own importance big,
  Disputing *which* most serves the nation.

Quoth Wig, with consequential air,
  " Pooh! pooh! you surely can't design,
My worthy beaver, to compare
  Your station in the state with mine.

" Who meets the learned legal crew?
  Who fronts the lordly Senate's pride?
The Wig, the Wig, my friend—while you
  Hang dangling on some peg outside.

" O, 'tis the Wig that rules, like Love,
  Senate and Court, with like *éclat* —
And wards below, and Lords above,
  For Law is Wig, and Wig is Law!"

" Who tried the long, *long* WELLESLEY suit,
  Which tried one's patience in return?

Not thou, O Hat! though, *couldst* thou do't,
   Of other *brims* than thine thou'dst learn.

"'Twas mine our master's toil to share,
   When, like 'Truepenny' in the play,
He every minute cried out, 'Swear,'
   And merrily to swear went they;—

"When, loth poor WELLESLEY to condemn, he
   With nice discrimination weigh'd,
Whether 'twas only 'Hell and Jemmy,'
   Or 'Hell and Tommy,' that he play'd.

"No, no, my worthy beaver, no;
   Though cheapen'd at the cheapest hatter's,
And smart enough, as beavers go,
   Thou ne'er wert made for public matters."

Here Wig concluded his oration,
   Looking, as wigs do, wondrous wise;
While thus, full cock'd for declamation,
   The veteran Hat, enrag'd, replies:

"Ho! dost thou then so soon forget
   What thou, what England owes to me?
Ungrateful Wig! when will a debt,
   So deep, so vast, be owed to thee?

"Think of that night, that fearful night,
  When through the steaming vault below
Our master dar'd, in gout's despite,
  To venture his podagric toe!

" Who was it then, thou boaster, say,
  When thou hadst to thy box sneak'd off,
Beneath his feet protecting lay,
  And sav'd him from a mortal cough?

" Think, if catarrh had quench'd that sun,
  How blank this world had been to thee!
Without that head to shine upon,
  O Wig, where would thy glory be?

" You, too, ye Britons—had this hope
  Of Church and State been ravish'd from ye,
O, think how Canning and the Pope
  Would then have played up 'Hell and Tommy'!

" At sea, there's but a plank, they say,
  'Twixt seamen and annihilation;
O Hat, that awful moment lay
  'Twixt England and Emancipation!

" Oh!!!—"

          At this Oh!! *The Times* reporter
Was taken poorly and retir'd;

Which made him cut Hat's rhetoric shorter
  Than justice to the case requir'd.

On his return, he found these shocks
  Of eloquence all ended quite;
And Wig lay snoring in his box,
  And Hat was—hung up for the night.

THE CASE ALTERED.

HODGE held a farm, and smiled content
While one year paid another's rent;
But if he ran the least behind
Vexation stung his anxious mind;
For not an hour would landlord stay,
But seize the very quarter day;
How cheap soe'er or scant the grain,
Though urged with truth, was urged in vain,
The same to him if false or true,
For rent must come when rent was due.
Yet that same landlord's cows and steeds
Broke Hodge's fence, and crops his meads;
In hunting, that same landlord's hounds,
See how they spread his new-sown grounds;
Dog, horse, and man, alike o'erjoyed,
While half the rising crop's destroyed,
Yet tamely was the loss sustain'd;
'Tis said the sufferer once complain'd;
The squire laugh'd loudly while he spoke,
And paid the bumpkin with a joke.

But luckless still, poor Hodge's fate!
His worship's bull has forced a gate,

And gored his cow, the last and best;
By sickness he had lost the rest.
Hodge felt at heart resentment strong—
The heart will feel that suffers long.
A thought that instant took his head,
And thus within himself he said :
" If Hodge for once don't sting the squire,
May people post him for a liar."
He then across his shoulder throws
His fork, and to his landlord goes.
"I come, an' please ye, to unfold
What soon or late you must be told :
My bull (a creature tame till now)—
My bull has gored your worship's cow.
'Tis known what shifts I make to live—
Perhaps your honor may forgive—no more.
" Forgive ! " the squire replied, and swore;
" Pray, cant to me forgive, no more !
The laws my damage shall decide,
And know that I'll be satisfied."
" Think, sir, I'm poor, poor as a rat."
" Think, I'm a justice, think of that."
Hodge bow'd again, and scratch'd his head,
And recollecting, archly said :
"Sir, I'm so struck when here before ye,
I fear I blundered in the story;

'Fore George! but I'll not blunder now,
Yours was the bull, sir; mine the cow!"
His worship found his rage subside,
And with calm accent thus replied:
"I'll think upon your case to-night,
But I perceived 'tis altered quite!"
Hodge shrugg'd, and made another bow,
" An' please ye, who's the Justice now?"

SETTLEMENT CASES.

SHADWELL *v.* ST. JOHNS WAPPING.

A WOMAN, having a settlement,
    Married a man with none.
The question was, he being dead,
    If that she had was gone?

Quoth Sir John Pratt: " Her settlement
    SUSPENDED did remain,
Living the husband. But, him dead,
    it doth *revive* again."

Chorus of Puisne Judges:
    "Living the husband; but, him dead,
    It doth revive again."

REX *v.* INHABITANTS OF ST. BOTOLPH'S.

A woman, having a settlement,
    Married a man with none;
He flies and leaves her destitute;
    What then is to be done?

Quoth Ryder, the chief justice:
    "In spite of Sir John Pratt,

You'll send her to the parish
In which she was a brat.

" *Suspension of a settlement*
Is not to be maintained;
That which she had by birth subsists
Until another's gained."

Chorus of Puisne Judges :
" That which she had by birth subsists
Until another's gained."

PUNCH IN CHANCERY.

REPORTED BY HIMSELF.

THE Court is crowded—on the bench is seen
England's Vice-Chancellor, with brow serene;
Within the bar silk-gownsmen strongly muster,
While in back rows the juniors thickly cluster—
Hoping some miracle may perhaps have sent
A stray half-guinea motion to consent;
But few, alas! are destined yet to see
Even the color of the casual fee.
Now, from the foremost bench, behold arise
A learned man—in counsel truly wise;
Sensation through the throng'd assembly ran,
As thus this learned counsellorbegan :
'Your Honor "—for 'tis thus old customs teach
The counsel to begin the legal speech—
"Your Honor, I've the honor to appear
For one whose fame extends from sphere to sphere;
The hero of the cap, the staff, the hunch,
The dog, the bell, the gallows—glorious PUNCH!
Vile arts some caitiff publisher pursues,
The fame of PUNCH to sully and abuse,
By pirating his form and brow serene,
Giving his countenance to things unclean."

No more the learned man had cause to speak,
For indignation blanched his Honor's cheek.
"Shall Punch," said he, " be thus dishonored?—O,
Thus from the judgment-seat, I answer—No.
Are caitiff publishers without compunction?
Take, Mr. Bethell—take a strong injunction.
And never did the Court commence the day
In such a jovial and auspicious way.
And thus, between its breakfast and its lunch,
Taking such very well-concocted Punch."
His Honor's joke caught by the eager bar,
Was duly welcomed by the loud " Ha, ha!"
" Silence!" the startled usher loudly call'd,
By such unusual sounds in court appall'd;
And strove, at first, to check the unheard-of din
Of chancery suitors yielding to a grin;
But soon his muscles, like dissolving lead,
Into a limpid smile are seen to spread;
While laughter's liquid fruits appear to rise
In liquid streamlets from his languid eyes.
Then Punch, obtaining all his counsel sought,
Departs triumphant from th' admiring court.

LAW OF HUSBAND AND WIFE.

SUPERIOR COURT, MAY TERM, 1837.

THE STATE *v.* HENRY DAY.

> *Semble*, that if A kills his bride,
> Such killing is not suicide.
>
> *Baron and feme* are only one,
> If any ill the wife hath done;
> If any crime the man doth do,
> *Baron and feme* are clearly two.
>
> In either case, or one or two,
> The *baron* must the penance do.

'Tis the hour of ten,
And a crowd of men
Wait at the door of the Justice Hall—
Bailiffs and suitors and jurors and all;
And a murmur loud
Runs thro' that crowd,
And ev'ry man gives his neighbor a nudge,
And all of them mutter, "Here comes the judge."

The passage is clear'd,
And the judge has appear'd;

21

A mild-looking man with a youthful face,
He strides up the hall, and he takes his place;
With "Silence!" the crowded hall resounds,
But not another note the curious list'ner wounds.

The sheriff "Oh yes! Oh yes!" hath bawl'd,
The witnesses come, and the jurors are call'd;
"Let the pris'ner be brought";
'Tis done, quick as thought;
A pale little man with a twinkling eye,
And an Amazon standing his shoulder by.
"Let the charge now be read."
'Tis done, quick as said.
"The jurors of this county town
Do, thro' their foreman, Moses Brown,
Charge and accuse that Henry Day,
Upon the seventh of this May,
Not having law before his eyes,
But urg'd on to the crying evil,
By sore seduction of the devil
(That hoary father of all lies),
Did bruise and wound and badly beat
His present wife, late Julia Sweet,
And other wrongs to his said mate,
All *contra pacem* of the State;
This is the charge against you brought,
Day, is it true, or is it not?"

The captive spake : " I own the strife,
I don't deny I struck my wife,
And for that part, where you aver,
The devil did my spirit stir,
'Tis true—for I was mov'd by her;
The dying sinner's wildest groans
Are music, to her gentlest tones,
And for her blows—alas, my bones!
Well, let it pass—perhaps 'twas wrong,
But I had borne her curses long,
And I am weak, and she is strong.
Let that too pass—I've done my best,
My counsel there must say the rest."

The pris'ner ceas'd.   His counsel rose,
He smoothed his hair, he blew his nose,
Then spake he : "If your honor please,
The points that mark this case are these,
This man has been from the beginning
Rather more sinn'd against than sinning;
'Tis hard to bear a woman's strife,
E'en if that woman be your wife;
'Tis hard to have a wife at all,
Yet not for that your grace, I call;
If we admit the deed was done,
Yet man and wife are only one;

And though we've read of many a fool,
Train'd up in superstition's school,
Who penance for his errors found
In many a self-inflicted wound,
Yet in no court beneath the sun
Hath he for that more penance done;
Tho' we despise the stupid elf,
He has a right to whip himself."
He ceas'd. 'Tis far the safest way
When one has nothing left to say.

Up rose the counsel for the State,
And thus kept up the sage debate:
" My learned brother's legal ground
Is far more specious, sir, than sound,
'Tis true, so doth the proverb run,
That " man and wife are only one,"
But 'tis a fiction of the law,
Not meant to cover baron's flaw.
Suppose in matrimonial strife
That A should stab and slay his wife,
My learned brother must agree
That this is not *felo de se;*
The facts are own'd—the law is clear,
And he his punishment must bear."

Now speaks the judge, in accents loud and clear,
Whilst not another sound disturbs the list'ning ear.
"I'll not detain the jury long;
The counsel is both right and wrong.
If any ill the wife hath done,
The man is fin'd—for they are one;
If any crime the man doth do,
Still he is fin'd—for they are two;
The rule is hard, it is confessed,
It can't be helped—*lex ita est.*"

'Let the passage be cleared."
The crowd disappear'd.
"Now call me the chief of the bailiffs here:
Sheriff, let it be thy care,
That this jury do not see
Food or drink 'till they agree;
(Woe to thee, if but one word
From other lips by them is heard.)
Be it thine especial charge
That they go no more at large
Until they notify to thee
That in this matter they agree.
Go, if thou abuse thy power,
Thy fate is fix'd this very hour!"

Again
'Tis ten;
Once more I sought that hall,
The judge look'd cross—the bailiffs crabbed,
The clerk and sheriff almost rabid,
For why? They had not slept at all:
And he, the chief of the bailiffs there,
Who had taken the jury under his care,
Look'd thirsty and vex'd as a wounded bear.
O, if the mother, that man that bore
Had seen him there at that jury door,
She never had known her offspring more.

What sound comes forth from the jury room,
Is it a curse,
Or something worse,
Or some poor devil bewailing his doom;
Or can it be the fearful cry
Of hungry juror's agony?
'Tis whisper'd around,
That no verdict is found,
That the jury in vain have sought to agree,
That some think *her* as much to blame as he,
And both to blame exceedingly.

I came away,
Thro' that justice door,

I've never seen Day,
From that time more;
I would not be willing to say or swear,
That those bailiffs and jurors are not still there;
But this I can tell,
For I know it full well,
That when last thro' that justice hall I pass'd,
The jury their food and drink were missing,
While the made-up pair were feasting and kissing.[3]

MORAL AND SEQUEL.

Jove laughs at lovers' vows and shame,
And men had better do the same.[4]

COOPER *VS.* BLOODGOOD.

32 N. J. Eq. 209.

Cooper foreclosed a mortgage made by Bloodgood
upon land,
A part whereof was river bank, and part was tidal
strand.
Complainant's assignor conveyed, by deed of war-
ranty
And covenant, that he had full right to grant the
same in fee,
And make the title to extend to mean low-water
mark;
And so such deed was drawn up by the scrivener
or his clerk.

This was infringing State domain, because, as you
can see,
The courts declared high-water line the limit of the
fee;
And when the time to answer came, why, the defendant, he
Put into the complainant's bill a Strong protesting
plea,

And said the title was not good to such a part of
    that

As was but water at high tide, at low tide a mud
    flat.

He was an oyster fisherman, and bought the property

For purposes connected with that kind of fishery;

And he had made improvements there, and spent a
    lot of " tin "

In building slips and wharves to keep his boats and
    bivalves in.

So as his grantor had conveyed the waters of the
    State,

He was advised to go and see the man who was the
    great,

Head-centre of " riprarian " rights, who told him
    that in law

. His lunar title was not worth an oyster shell or
    straw.

Then he took out a lease, just as prescribed by stat-
    ute rule,

For which he pays an annual rent, to help the pub-
    lic school:

His lawyer told him not to pay the mortgage he
    had made,

Without offsetting what he had for such improve-
    ments paid;

And so he did decline to give complainant what
     seemed due
Upon the bond and mortgage, marked Exhibits One
     and Two.
Wherefore from hence to be dismissed, with costs,
     he now would pray,
And be decreed in equity, to go without a day.

Complainant urged defendant was an expert oyster-
     man,
And well acquainted with the laws of rights
     ripari-an.
Besides, he said, I have here now, and show you,
     worthy sirs,
A license issued by the board of chosen freehold-ers,
Being a document herein of vital pith and core,
And by the master in this cause marked as Exhibit
     Four,
Because it was a part of the conditions of the sale,
And shows the tidal grant did not in any aspect fail;
It was besides an older grant than said riparian lease,
And from that lunar document knocked every spot
     of grease.
From all of which, complainant says, it plainly now
     appears
Defendant had the right to build docks, wharves,
     and slips and piers,

And having that, and knowing too just what he was
    about,
He cannot plead his mother did not know that he
    was out,
And ask relief to free him from the promise he had
    made,
By entering a decree herein, the debt should not be
    paid.

The Chancellor *advisare vult*, and then he says,
    says he,
Having considered, I adjudge, and order and decree,
Because from license, lease, and facts, it does appear
    to me,
The merits, law, and principle, justice, and equity
Of this riparian, lunar case are with the mortgagee,
And by assignment appertain unto his assignee,
As *vide* same marked in this cause Exhibit No.
    Three;
Defendant was familiar with riparian tidal right,
And knew precisely what he took with land her-
    maphrodite;
All which appearing very plain and free from any
    doubt,
My judgment in the matter is—defendant must
    shell out.

The lawyers got their costs, and the complainant
    got the land,

And still a part is river bank, and part is tidal
    strand;

Aud standing on the bluff you see the sea at Sandy
    Hook

Across the waters, out of which the oyster-fish are
    took.

Hence oyster fisherman may learn this lesson from
    the rule,

Don't take out a riparian lease, and don't be such
    a fool

To pay an annual interest to State or public school,

Until you are quite certain, and each surely
    re-mem-bers

No license had been issued by the chosen free-
    holders;

For if you do the two will cost in rent and taxes
    double,

And lease and license roll on you a tidal wave of
    trouble,

Lawyers will get the oyster, and it will be mighty
    well

If you get one, and t'other man the other oyster
    shell.

CRAFT *VS.* BOITE.

London, to wit: Hereby complains
　One Joseph Craft, a clerk in orders,
Of Joseph Boite, in custody
　Within the marshal's bounds and borders.

For Craft, a worthy man is he;
　A loyal subject always reckoned,
Both of the Lord King Charles the First,
　And of the Lord King Charles the Second.

Unhurt, untouched, immaculate,
　A man renowned for godly labors,
Good, honest, pious, faithful, true,
　He had the love of all his neighbors.

And eke by venerable folk
　Esteemed he was of good condition;
And as to theft and felony,
　Devoid of blame, above suspicion.

Yea, more: great gains he daily had,
　And profits highly advantageous;
(Indeed, to slander such a man
　Would be appallingly outrageous.)

22

Yet him contriving to defame,
　　Though all the premises well knowing,
Came Joseph Boite, this righteous clerk
　　Into contempt in public throwing.

Loud in the English tongue he spoke,
　　With voice enough to raise a Quaker:
"Saw'st ever such a thievish rogue
　　As young Joe Craft, the silver-taker?"

And then, with index-digit raised,
　　" See there! to my most certain knowledge
He stole two hundred pounds of plate—
　　Did Joseph Craft from Wadham College!"

And once again in London town
　　(The repetition sadly shocks one):
"There never was a thievish rogue
　　Like Joseph Craft, of Wadham, Oxon!"

Whereas, the thing was false and feigned,
　　A scandalous insinuation,
Whereby the plaintiff is annoyed
　　And injured in his reputation.

And divers subjects of the king,
　　Supposing him bereft of piety,

Have now withdrawn, and more and more
   Withdraw themselves from his society.
*   *   *   *   *
And now when Hilary is past,
   The days of his imparlance ending,
To Westminster came Joseph Boite,
   The wrong and injury defending.

For since the words he spoke were all
   As true as any text in Bible,
Because the plaintiff stole the plate,
   There could not be a civil libel.
*   *   *   *   *
And Craft, for replication, says
   Defendant spoke these words misleading
Of his own wrong, without such cause
   As he (said Boite) alleged in pleading.

What was the tale about the plate?
   From first to last a fabrication.
It was a scandal false and famed,
   A lie without the least foundation.
*   *   *   *   *
Within a month of Easter-tide,
   In ermined pomp, his rank befitting,
The well-belov'd John Kelynge, Knight,
   Was in the chair of judgment sitting.

And now, in conscious justice, Craft
    Was waiting for his credit's clearance;
But wicked Boite, in solemn form
    Though thrice invoked, made no appearance.

Wherefore the plaintiff soon was seen
    As proud and gay as Harry Percy,
With damages and costs in pouch;
    " And the said Joseph Boite in mercy."

PUNCH'S LAW REPORTS.

The Great Ham Case.— REGINA *v.* GALLARS.

THE case it was this : There was tried at the Ses-
    sions
A prisoner, guilty of divers transgressions ;
And wishing at last for a relishing cram,
His career he had finished by stealing a ham.
At the trial objection was made—that the joint
Had been badly described—and reserved was the
    point.
For the prisoner : HENNIKER rose in his place,
To contend the proceedings were bad on their face.
He urged "that the article now in dispute
Had been very likely a bit of a brute,
An animal, *feræ naturæ*, whose hocks
Had been made into ham (see the QUEEN *versus*
    Cox),
Where some eggs had been stolen, and there 'twas
    laid down,
The indictment was bad on the part of the Crown,
Because of the eggs 'twas not plainly averr'd,
Whether those of a crocodile, adder, or bird."
Per POLLOCK, Chief Baron : "The question one begs,
In refusing to recognize eggs, sir, as eggs ;

I'm convinced such objection could never be made
As to hold that an egg was improperly laid."
Per PATTERSON, Justice : " The point I see well,
For the whole of the argument lies in the shell."
But suppose with the eggs there had been an as-
    sault,
Will you venture to tell us that justice must halt
If the egg's undescribed ? On your law I can't flat-
    ter ye ;
To call it an egg is sufficient in battery."
Per PLATT, Puisne Baron : " Suppose, for a change,
An epicure fancies a dish somewhat strange.
And orders the ham of a fox or a rat,
There'd then be a property surely in that ?"
MR. HENNIKER humbly submitted that dogs,
Whom he ventured to couple, in this case, with
    hogs
(He made no reflection, and wished not to pass any),
Had become very recently subjects of larceny.
Per PLATT: " But the law, sir, had always its eye
On a toad in the hole, or a dog in a pie."
The learned Chief Baron conferred with the judges,
Who declared the objection the poorest of fudges.
The pris'ner's conviction accordingly stood ;
The ham and indictment were both pronounced
    good.

LEWIS *VS.* STATE.

SYLLABUS.

Law—Paw—Guilt—Wilt.

When upon thy frame the law
Places its majestic paw,
Though in innocence or guilt,
Thou art then required to wilt.

STATEMENT OF CASE BY REPORTER.

THIS defendant, while at large,
Was arrested on a charge
Of burglarious intent,
And direct to jail he went.
But he somehow felt misused,
And through prison walls he oozed,
And in some unheard-of shape
He effected his escape.

Mark you, now: Again the law
On defendant placed its paw,
Like a hand of iron mail.
And resocked him into jail—
Which said jail, while so corralled,
He by sockage, tenure held.

Then the Court met, and they tried
Lewis up and down each side,
On the good old-fashioned plan;
But the jury cleared the man.

Now, *you* think that this strange case
Ends at just about this place.
Nay, not so. Again the law
On defendant placed its paw.
This time takes him round the cape
For effecting an escape;
He, unable to give bail,
Goes reluctantly to jail.

Lewis, tried for this last act,
Makes a special plea of fact:
"Wrongly did they me arrest,
As my trial did attest,
And while rightfully at large,
Taken on a wrongful charge
I took back from them what they
From me wrongly took away."

When this special plea was heard
Thereupon the State demurred.

The defendant then was pained
When the Court was heard to say.

In a cold, impassive way,
" The demurrer is sustained."

Back to jail did LEWIS go,
But as liberty was dear,
He appeals, and now is here
To reverse the judge below.
The opinion will contain
All the statements that remain.

ARGUMENT AND BRIEF OF APPELLANT.

As a matter, sir, of fact,
Who was injured by our act,
Any property, or man ?
Point it out, sir, if you can.
Can you seize us when at large,
On a baseless, trumped-up charge ;
And if we escape, then say
It is *crime* to get away—
When we rightfully regain'd
What was wrongfully obtained ?

Please—the—Court—sir, what is crime ?
What is right, and what is wrong ?
Is our freedom but a song,
Or the subject of a rhyme ?

ARGUMENT AND BRIEF OF ATTORNEY FOR THE
STATE.

When the STATE, that is to say,
 We take liberty away—
When the padlock and the hasp
Leaves one helpless iu our grasp
It's unlawful then that he
Even *dreams* of liberty—
Wicked dreams that may in time
Grow and ripen into *crime*—
Crime of dark and damning shape ;
Then, if he perchance escape,
Evermore remorse will roll
O'er his shattered, sin-sick soul.
Please—the—Court—sir, how can we,
Manage people who get free ?

REPLY OF APPELLANT.

Please—the—Court—sir, if it's *sin,*
Where does *turpitude* begin ?

OPINION OF THE COURT.   PER CURIAM.

We—don't—make—law: we are bound
To interpret it as found.

The defendant broke away :
When arrested, he should stay.

This appeal can't be maintained,
For the record does not show
Error in the Court below,
   And we nothing can infer.
Let the judgment be sustained :
   All the justices concur.

NOTE BY THE REPORTER.

Of the Sheriff, rise and sing,
" Glory to our earthly King ! "

KUHN ET AL. *VS.* JEWETT, Receiver.

32 N. J. Eq. 647.

The shades of night were falling fast,
As o'er the Erie Railroad passed
A locomotive, laden down
With crude petroleum, near the town
     Of Paterson.

A piercing shriek, a blinding flash,
And then an instantaneous crash—
Two trains collided—down the banks
The oil was emptied from the tanks
     Immediately.

The oil igniting, sparkling, flowed
Down the embankment, across the road,
Into a bubbling brook that pours
Its waters on the fertile shores
     Of the Passaic.

The barn of the complainants stood
Beside this unheroic flood.
And thus the floating flames of fire
Consumed it, and produced a dire
     Calamity.

His Honor, the Vice-Chancellor, says
That if a devastating blaze
Is negligently started, still
Defendant is responsible
In damages.

If no obstructions intervene,
As a new agency, between '
The cause and its effect, as here;
This rule is singularly clear
And logical.

23

CUSHING *VS.* BLAKE

29 N. J. Eq. 399; 30 N. J. Eq. 689.

SIR MARMADUKE, about to wed,
　　Some profitable lands conveyed
In trust unto Antonio,
　　To hold them for his spouse's aid.

To give unto her separate use
　　Their issues and emoluments,
Their profits, perquisites, proceeds,
　　And all their revenue and rents.

And for a further trust convey
　　To whomsoever she'd require,
By writing in her life, or else
　　By testament should she expire;

No disposition being made
　　By writing or by testament,
To go unto her heirs at law
　　As per the statutes of descent.

Sir Marmaduke was wed, but lo!
　　The lady of his love declined,
And died possessed of all her lands,
　　But left a baby boy behind.

Sir Marmaduke now filed a bill,
  And the Chancellor held, in his decree,
The estate of Mrs. Marmaduke
  An equitable one in fee.

The trust was executed, not
  A trust executory, so
The rule in Shelley's case directs
  The manner that the lands shall go.

And on appeal, the Court above
  Affirmed the Chancellor's decree,
And so Sir Marmaduke obtained
  His equitable courtesy.

COMMONWEALTH *VS.* McAFEE.

108 Mass. 458.

Hugh McAfee, of Boston town,
  Claimed, that, at common law,
He had the right, when she was drunk,
  To beat his wife therefor.
As a defense, he claimed it,
  Upon his trial day,
And swore his wife was insolent,
And when he struck, he never meant
  To take her life away.

Then out spake Reuben Chapman,
  Chief Justice of the Court:
"To every woman in this State
  Life may be long or short;
But while I hold this office,
  No woman in this land
Shall lawfully be beaten
  By her husband's brutal hand."

Hugh McAfee, the husband, was
  Convicted of manslaughter;
And thus the everlasting right,
  To every wife and daughter,

By brave old Reuben Chapman's act,
   Was given on that day,
To get drunk and be insolent,
   Free from a husband's sway.

OPINION OF JUSTICES.

106 Mass. 604.

WOMAN! thy mission is to please:
Not to be Justice of the Peace;
Content with what the laws allow,
A school-committee woman thou!

LUTHER *VS.* WORCESTER.

97 Mass. 272.

In Worcester, when the sun was low,
Trodden in ridges lay the snow ;
Across the walk he tried to go,
But fell, tho' walking carefully.

Had Luther seen another sight,
Of sidewalk smooth with ice that night,
Without a ridge thereon, he might
Have suffered, without remedy.

The Court this plain distinction draw:
" When ice and snow, by natural law,
Are slippery found before your door,
You fall—the town's not liable.

" But when by man they're trodden down
In ridges, or an icy crown,
You, falling then, can sue the town,
And get your heavy damages."

THE LAD FRAE COCKPEN.

'Twas a lad frae Cockpen; he was proud and was
    great,
His mind was ta'en up wi' the married estate,
He had but ae wife, so he wanted anither,
For he said his auld wife might be almost his
    mither.

So he met wi' a lass, did this lad frae Cockpen,
And what was his errand he soon let her ken;
The answer she gied it is easy to guess,
She swithered a wee, and then she said, "Yes."

This young Irish lass (she was Irish, ye see),
To gie her due credit she swithered a wee;
It's a trick of the trade just to tickle the men,
It's a way they've in Ireland as weel as Cockpen.

This new-married pair dwelt in the Green Isle,
And happy they lived there—at least for a while,
Till the thing spunkit out—it's a way *it* has, then
Who appears on the scene but the wife frae Cock-
    pen.

He was ta'en up and tried 'fore the wise Baron
    Deasy,
And at first he took it remarkably aisy;
But he got his five years, and 'twas added that ten
Would be little enough for this lad frae Cockpen.

Then (of course) he was seized wi' a sudden remorse,
Said, "I'd raither been tried by the Laird of Glen-
    corse";
And he sighed in his cell, where there's nae but
    and ben,
"I was daft to desert my auld wife in Cockpen."

OWEN KERR *VS.* OWEN KERR.

If the strife in this case is extremely perverse,
'Tis because 'tis between a couple of "Kerrs."
Each Owen is owin'—but here lies the bother:
To determine which Owen is owin' the other.
Each Owen swears Owen to Owen is owin',
And each alike certain, dog-matic, and knowin';
But 'tis hoped that the jury will not be deterred
From finding which "Kerr" the true debt has
      incurred;
Thus settling which Owen by *owin'* has failed,
And that justice 'twixt curs has not been *cur*tailed.

CONTRIBUTORY NEGLIGENCE.

Tuff v. Warman, 5 C. B. N. S. 573.

Ingenuous student, who with curious eye
Would trace the tangled threads of thought that lie
Involved in oracles of *Tuff and Warman,*
Hear, on that well-thumb'd text, a homely sermon.
The text, though cumbered much with clause on
    clause,
Reads fairly plain, till near an end it draws;
But at the end, through devious ways, we come
To rule that gravels pleaders, all and some.
Here Wightman, Justice, tells us, in effect,
Plaintiff stands none the worse of 's own neglect,
If but Defendant, when default is made,
Its consequences could with care evade.
The canon at first blush reads all too wide,
Unless a triple caution be supplied;
Which to supply, and point you out the way,
To find where wanted, here, in loyal lay,
Contributory Negligence I sing,
The rule of Law, and reason of the thing.

Both are in fault: else—'tis a simple story—
The negligence were not contributory.

Then, either both have been in fault together,
Or else the one's in fault before the other.
If both together, neither bears the blame ;
The wrongs concurrent, and the rights the same ;
If fault of one, the other's fault precede ;
He pays the penalty: unless, indeed,
The other, by some little common sense,
Could shun that first misconduct's consequence.

Say, I lie drunk, a trespasser besides,
On *Marcus'* avenue ; and *Marcus* rides
Or stumbles o'er me; still, first question is
(Be it the broken bones are mine or his),
Could *Marcus*, by an ordinary care,
Have shunned the danger, and so gone elsewhere ?
If *yea*, he pays me for my hurt; altho'
I was in act the first to blame ; if *no*,
Since but for me he ne'er had been o'erthrown,
I pay him for his hurt and bear my own.

What, then, whene'er by night I walk or ride,
Must I a link-boy or a scout provide,
Lest *Davies'* donkey in my path should roll,[1]
Or *Forrester* have left his building pole[2]

[1] Davies *v.* Mann, 10 M. & W. 546.
[2] Butterfield *v.* Forrester, 11 East. 60.

To trip me up? nay, Law was never heard
To sanction charge of caution so absurd.
I must not, if I'd not be brought to book,
Run blind-man's muck, and leap before I look;
(Though some that leap'd and never looked, have
     found
A verdict 'twixt the foot-board and the ground;)[3]
But if with eye-sight such as blessed withal,
I keep my head from contact with the wall
By ordinary care, the law demands
No weightier charge of caution at my hands.
But say I'm blind; or one of tender years,
Insensible to age's prudent fears?
Your case thereby nor better is nor worse,
Your leader answers for you, or your nurse.[4]

Of these collateral moot-points enough :
Return we now to *Warman* versus *Tuff*,
The judgment's truly neither less nor more
Than, done in dogg'rel, is set down before;—
One's first in fault; then, could the other one
That fault's effects by common caution shun?
But there you stop; else, caught in Pleader's Pound.
Each cries, *Tu quoque!* in an endless round.

[3] Scott *v.* Dublin & Wicklow Ry. Co. 11 W. C. L. R. 377.
[4] Lynch *v.* Nurdin, 4 P. & D. 672. Waite *v.* Nth. Ln. Ry.
Cov. 1 El. B. & E. 719.

As, say, that when, a log, in *Marcus'* way
By want of ordinary care I lay,
Marcus athwart me falling breaks his head,
And brings his suit; if, in defense, 'tis said,
' You might have shunned me, had you used your
      eyes ";
And *Marcus* then with Wightman, J., replies,
" And *you* shunned *me!*" the altercation tends
To circular dispute that never ends.[c]
Or, say two runners, each a careless spark,
Have clashed their heads together in the dark;
It lies not in the mouth of one to say,
" Sir, you by caution could have kept away,
And so I had not dashed and lost my tooth
'Gainst your *os frontis*"; for the other youth
With equal justice may in turn reply,
" Nor had *I* dashed 'gainst *yours*, and lost my eye."
For here the active fault of both concurr'd,
And left to neither, in the law, a word.[A]
Or say two barges insecurely moor'd
Drift in a stream, with neither crew on board:
Borne in an eddy of the wind or tide,
The barques approach, and with a crash collide;
My planks stove in afford as little room
For just complaint, as does *your* broken boom.
For here the passive fault of both together
Has shut the mouth of each against the other.[B]

24

But two, each so in fault, will yield no more
Predicaments of blame, but only four;[5]
And Wightman's canon, as above we see,
Holds not of these, in categories three;
.Wherefore his " Plaintiff's non-disabling fault "
Must needs be taken with three grains of salt,
And limited to that one category,
Where Plaintiff's fault's the first contributory.
As if, say last, when *Marcus* o'er me rode,
Broad daylight had the present danger show'd,
And I, as plaintiff, my crushed ribs had mourn'd
Whereto " *Tu quoque* " *Marcus* had return'd.
Then, in that case, but in that only one,
May I reply as Wightman, J., has done,
" True, 'twas my first default that brought me there,
But you, good *Marcus,* could, with common care,
Have shunned me where I lay, and in that state
Of things, 'tis lawful to recriminate.[D]

By Wightman's judgment, then, 'twas never meant
That Plaintiff's negligence should not prevent
Plaintiff's success, in any of the three
Firstly above-put cases: Wherefore, ye

[5] Viz., Negligence in both,	Concurrent,	Both active.[A]
		Both passive.[B]
	Non-concurrent,	Plff. act.; dft. pass.[C]
		Plff. pass.: dft. act.[D]

Who scan that clause so oft misunderstood,
Read, " If defendant by due caution could
(*When Plaintiff has been first to blame, in fact*)
Have shunned the consequence of Plaintiff's act,
The Plaintiff shall not thereby be undone."
So shall the Law and Judgment be at one.

HOPKINS *VS.* W. P. R. R. CO.

" Cacata charta."—CATULLUS.

In Stockton town did plaintiff hold
  A tract of land in fee,
And on it, in a goodly house,
  Dwelt with his family.
Thought he, " Though but to utter edge
  Doth run this lot of mine,
Yet do I own the street unto
  The highway's middle line." [1]

So at his gate if idler stayed,
  Or small boy paused to scoff,
Secure in his allodial rights,
  The plaintiff warned them off.
And when the shades of evening fell,
  With hose and spanner gay,
He strode before his castle gate,
  And flooded all the way.[2]

---

[1] See sec. 1112, Civil Code; see also Washburn on Real
Property, vol. iii. p. 420 *et seq.*; also Washburn, Easements
and Servitudes, p. 228.

[2] The reader will note with pleasure the deft manner in
which the poet has set forth the customary seignorial acts
done by the freeholder upon his land. Is there any right enjoyed by the average citizen with more zest than that of wet-

O, happy is that baron's soul
    Who hath both feme and home !
O, happy such abode where naught
    Of force or wrong may come !
Secure the proud freeholder sits,
    Seized as of his demesne—
(At least, where'er the common law,
    As here, doth most obtain).[1]

He knoweth joys that ne'er can know
    The poor, wayfaring man,
Sojourning here and there in spots,
    'Neath landlords' grievous ban—
His *lares* ever packed in trunks,
    His journey never done ;
But like Æneas—wretched fate !—
    Forever "moving on."[2]

ting down the street? The old privileges of *haute et basse justice, culagium, marchetum*, etc., etc., as enjoyed by the noblesse in old days (see *Droit du Seigneur*), are nothing as compared to the modern luxury of turning the hose upon the arid highway.

[1] It is needless to point out to the learned reader that every householding citizen in the United States is or ought to be a baron; although in California, out of delicate reverence to the departed glory of the Spanish sway, we might spell it *varon*. Of course every baron should have a castle.

[2] If the poet here had in his mind the good old hymn—
    "No foot of land do I possess,
    No cottage in this wilderness—
    A poor wayfaring man "—
he will be pardoned his evident plagiarism.

So weened the plaintiff at his ease,
　　As through his grounds he walked,
And with his sympathizing spouse
　　Confidingly he talked.
Alas!　But what is happiness?
　　'Tis but a fleeting breath;
'Tis, as the Grecian jurist said,
　　Uncertain eke to death.[1]

For lo!　A railway company—
　　Fierce, ruthless men were they—
Came like a scourge, condemning lands,
　　Demanding right of way.
And through the street by plaintiff's house
　　Their road-bed broad they laid,
And ballast brought, and all along
　　A steep embankment made.[2]

And that the winter rains might have
　　Some proper aqueduct,
Beneath their road a culvert there
　　They skillfully construct.

---

[1] It is proper here to claim Solon as a jurist, although he might be ranked as poet.

[2] See sec. 428, Code Civil Procedure, sub. 4; sec. 465, Civil Code, sub. 3, 4; see also Southern Pac. R. R. Co. v. Raymond, 53 Cal. 226.

'Twas done: that haunt of ancient peace
 Now quivers at the train;
That once calm street re-echoes sounds
 That beat into the brain.

The locomotive wheels along
 Like dragon fierce of yore,
While murky puffs of stifling smoke
 From out its nostrils pour.
And ever in the gladsome night,
 Its shriek breaks sharply in,
As though some Titan penance did
 For old chaotic sin.

'Twas such and many a grief beside
 The plaintiff suffered sore,
As by his hearth-stone, ash-besprent,
 A burdened life he bore.
If aught courageous could avail
 His peace thus sadly vexed—
But where to seek a remedy—
 'Twas that his brain perplexed.

For guileless heart the plaintiff had,
 Nor sought litigious fame,
And ne'er the thought of writs or suits
 In his reflections came.

But writhing worms will turn, 'tis said,
　　In the oppressor's track;
An added plume will sometimes break
　　The laden camel's back.

It thus befell: chance passers-by,
　　Or loiterers on the line,
That culvert cool did dedicate
　　To Venus Cloacine.
And often to the fragrant shrine
　　Did railway folks repair,
And leave, at Nature's warning call,
　　Their casual offerings there.[1]

And now that culvert, whence once quelled
　　But pure pellucid streams,
A poisoned den of rank disease,
　　With noisome odors steams.
And when fair Stockton's winds did rise
　　And through the culvert blow,

---

[1] In what way the ancient Romans effected a dedication of a temple to Venus Cloacina, the poet refers his readers to classical sources. The force of ancient paganism and its habits may be said to survive among us in the readiness with which old mining tunnels and other deserted excavations are, throughout the mining districts of California and Nevada, consecrated promptly to Venus or Idalian Aphrodite, under her epithet of Cloacina.

The plaintiff found what potent power
  They had to work him woe.

Then bursts his rage, long smothered, forth,
  Flames up each burning grudge,
And up he starts in direful heat
  To seek his District Judge.
*   *   *   *   *
A panel struck—all neighbors kind—
  They piteous grant redress,
When duly charged by Booker, J.,
  His damage to assess.

The plaintiff seeks his home content,
  A victor from the field.
But finds, alas! the strife renewed—
  The scoundrels have appealed;
In sooth, these corporations have
  The might of gold in hand,
And of forensic bravos hold
  In pay a murd'rous band.[1]
*   *   *   *   *
The Transcript filed, the fees all paid,
  The cause came duly on;

---

[1] The kindly critical reader may think this verse is bathos.
He is right.

'Twas Budd forth for respondent stood,
  'Gainst surly Sanderson.
And now the bailiff opens court—
  Stilled is the vulgar hum,
While through the door, in ordered file.
  Their Honors gravely come.[1]

Note Wallace, he of saintly mien,
  Mark Crockett's gleeful air,
And Niles, whose pale and hollow checks
  Tell of his meager fare.
Anon the fiery Rhodes trips in;
  Behind him follows close
McKinstry, he whose wrinkled brow
  Betrays judicial throes.[2]

The case is called, and Sanderson
  Pooh-poohs respondent's woes,
And Budd replies, and to and fro
  The tide of warfare flows.
  *   *   *   *   *
Now doth the Court deliberate
  With many a hem and haw—

---

[1] If the poet here drops into a dramatic style and a historical present, it is because he is carried away by the flow of rhythm.

[2] The keenness with which the poet has hit off the salient characteristics of their Honors will be duly appreciated by the bar.

Agreed at last—McKinstry, J.,
　Expounds the nuisance law :

" *Non constat* that the company
　All those rude men employed,
Who in said culvert casements have
　Thus cozily enjoyed.
And *semble,* when the employés
　Did 'neath the archway grope,
Not all their movements sejant were
　In their employment's scope.

" And too, it should be ranked among
　Most clear-admitted facts,
That such as must be corporal
　Can scarce be corporate acts.
A corporation ever works
　Through its attorneys leal,
Nor cravings purely physical
　Can it be deemed to feel.

"'Tis whispered children are begot
　At times by proxies' means
(Though to dispense with agents' aids
　The general custom leans).
But who would blow another's nose,
　Or sneeze another's sneeze,

Or do vicariously such acts
  As give our bodies ease?

"So of our legal knot, in this
  The true solution lies:
The trespassers were but engaged
  In privy enterprise.
And since such easements scarce are deemed
  Rights incorporeal,
'Gainst each, for trespass, plaintiff might
  Have action several.

"Of turbary and piscary,
  A common there may be,
And in one action all be sued
  To reach a remedy;
But here, 'twould seem, th' offenders sought
  The culvert one by one,
And had their musings, Crusoe-like,
  Unsocial and alone.

"So while the learned judge below
  We hold in high esteem,
Erroneous, in this one case,
  His rulings we do deem.
We therefore hold it to be law
  In this our *curia*,

If plaintiff's damaged, damned he is
    Absque injuria."

His Honor ceased: a wail of woe
    Burst from respondent's throat;
He rushed abroad, and started home
    For Stockton by the boat.
But where the Sacramento's floods
    Thy shores, San Pablo, lave,
He leaped into the rushing tide
    To find a peaceful grave.[1]

And now, when trains through Stockton town
    Are passing in the night,
A wraith is said to haunt the track,
    And vex the stoker's sight.
And if unto that culvert now
    A hasty soul retreats,
Before his frightened gaze a form
    Uncertain glares and fleets.[2]

---

[1] The neat way in which the poet has here imitated Virgil, in his address to lake Benacus, will be appreciated by every true Virgilian scholar:

      " Fluctibus et fremitu assurgens, Benace, marino."

[2] We hope and believe that the estimable gentleman who figured as respondent in the above case is still alive, and enjoying existence where no railway corporation can trample on his rights. The poet has murdered him, only in accordance with true rules of art, to bring in the tragic element which in actuality we trust he may never have any connection with.

25

TRUX APER INSEQUITUR.

APPEAL—M'VEY *vs.* HENNIGAN.

TUNE—"Judy Callaghan."

THERE lived, as I am tould,
  In Stirling's noble city,
Two Irish lads so bould,
  The subjec' av me ditty;
They both had pigs galore,
  And styes to fence and screen 'em,
And each possessed a boar,
  With only a hedge between 'em.
        Says M'Vey—
    Darlint Mr. Hennigan,
    You must pay
    If your boar comes in again.

Tony Hennigan's boar,
  Faix, he loved to wandher;
Divvel a wall or door
  Would kape him from his dandher.
And mostly he would hie
  To Pat M'Vey's back garden,
And grunt about the stye
  Where Pathrick's pigs were barred in.

Says M'Vey—
Darlint Mr. Hennigan,
You must pay
If your boar comes in again.

At last one day when Pat
   Was atin' av his dinner,
His wife cried out, "Ther's that
   Ould boar, as I'm a sinner.
O Pat, rise up, make haste,"
   And Pat obeyed her ordhers,
And swore he'd drive the baste
   From out his garden bordhers.
     Says M'Vey—
   Darlint Mr. Hennigan,
   You must pay
   Now your boar's come in again.

But Tony's boar, worse luck,
   He had a heart so darin',
Bedad! he run amuck
   At this bould son av Erin.
So Pat was forced to fly,
   And moighty quick he went too,
While Piggy from his thigh
   Tore out a small memento.

                        Says M'Vey—
        Darliut Mr. Hennigan,
        You must pay
        Now your boar's come in again.

Then Pathrick to the Coort
    He dhragged the porker's masther,
And swore that such a hurt
    Bank notes alone could plasther.
The stye was insecure,
    The boar was most fherocious,
And Tony's conduct, shure,
    Was blackgyard and athrocious.
                        Says M'Vey—
        Darlint Mr. Hennigan,
        You must pay
        Now your boar's come in again.

Me piggy has, says Tone,
    The swatest, best of naytures,
And Pat, ye should have known
    The ways av them dumb craytures;
His timper's asily stirred,
    When takin' av his airin',
Nor can he stand a worrd
    Av cursin' or av swearin'!

Says M'Vey—
Darlint Mr. Hennigan,
You must pay
Now your boar's come in again.

Upon the case there sat
  Two sheriffs, larnéd brothers,
One gave his vote for Pat,
  And Tony got the other's.
And so when months had passed
  In strife and opposition,
The case was brought at last
  Before the Coort av Session.
                  Says M'Vey—
Darlint Mr. Hennigan,
You must pay
Now your boar's come in again.

The Lords, in gowns so grand,
  Were tould the dismal story
How piggy, though so bland,
  Made Pathrick's groin so gory;
They said 'twas not polite
  For Pat to use such langwidge,
Still Piggy had no right
  To ate a raw ham sandwich!

Says M'Vey—
Darlint Mr. Hennigan,
You must pay
Now your boar's come in again.

Then nivver, if you're wise,
  Permit your pigs, be jabers!
To threspass on the thighs
  Av your Milesian neighbours.
For boars whose moral sinse
  Is shocked by imprecation,
Are apt to take offince
  At all the Irish nation.
        Says M'Vey—
    Darlint Mr. Hennigan,
    You must pay
    Now your boar's come in again.

NOTES

AND REFERENCES.

———

The numbers refer to the pages on which the verses are found.

———

11. A Lawyer's Farewell to His Muse. By Sir William Blackstone Knight. There is a certain quaint awkwardness in the great commentator's rhymes which show that he had grudgingly bestowed his attention upon verse while cultivating as clear and harmonious a prose style as our language is capable of fostering. See Roscoe's Life for this and the succeeding piece, "The Lawyer's Prayer," by the learned Knight.

18. A Flight of Fancy. By Frances Sargent Osgood. See her "Poems," 12 mo, p. 31.

23. Ode to a Sparrow.

26. On the Approach of Spring. *Punch*, Vol. XX. (1851), p. 144. By Tom Taylor, the well-known author and dramatist called to the bar as member of the Inner Temple in 1845, a frequent contributor to *Punch* and other periodicals of articles in prose and verse, author of "Our American Cousin." "Ticket of Leave Man," and many other dramas. See *Knickerbocker Magazine*, Vol. LIV., p. 103, credited in Bryant's "Library of Poetry and Song" to Henry Howard Brownell, but not contained in his volume "War Lyrics and Other Poems."

27. Sweet Autumn Days. *Punch*, Vol. I. (1841), p. 153.

28. A Professional Pastoral for the Long Vacation. *Punch*, Vol. VII. (1844), p. 148.

29. Trills for Term Time. *Punch*, Vol. XIII. (1847), p. 199.

30.　Response at Boston Bar Banquet.　By Dr. Oliver Wendell Holmes.　At the annual banquet of the Boston Bar Association in January, 1883, Hon. Wm. G. Russell, President, having offered toasts to the Courts and to the Mayor, said : —

"We are done with officials and public functionaries, and we come now to a tough subject; many-sided, and I know not on which side to attack him with any hope of capturing him. I might hail him as our poet, for he was born a poet; they are all born so. If he didn't lisp in numbers it was because he spoke plainly at a very early age. I might hail him as physician, and a long and well-spent life in that profession would justify it; but I don't believe it will ever be known whether he has cured more cases of dyspepsia and blues by his poems, or his powders and his pills. I might hail him as professor, and as professor *emeritus* he has added a new wreath to his brow. I might hail him as Autocrat of the Breakfast Table, for there he had a long reign, and he prolongs it at all our later repasts. He will defend himself with courage, for he never showed the white feather but once, and that is that he does not dare to be as funny as he can. A tough subject, surely, and I must try him on the tender side, the paternal. I give you the father who went in search of a captain, and, finding him, presents to us now his son the judge."

Dr. Holmes, on rising, held up a sheet of paper and said: "You see before you (referring to the paper) all that you have to fear or hope. For thirty-five years I have taught anatomy. I have often heard of the roots of the tongue, but I never found them. The danger of a tongue let loose you have had opportunity to know before, but the danger of a scrap of paper like this is so trivial that I hardly need to apologize for it." *Boston Evening Transcript,* January 31, 1883.

33.　Nonsuited.　By T. H. E. Printer.　Written to order to fill a page.

34.　The Special Pleader's Lament, appeared first in *The Jurist,* Vol. I., January 28, 1837, copied in *The American Jurist,* Vol. XXI., p. 239, afterwards appeared in 7 Robinson's Practice, p. 1095, with additional verse : —

> "But then, alas! the Barons held
> The transfer of this treasure
> Could not by me be set aside,
> Being made when *under pressure.*"

38.　Law Love, found in *The Western Jurist,* Vol. VIII., p. 181.

39. Lines to Bessie. By a student at law. *Punch*, Vol. VII. (1844), p. 58, gives these verses with the following characteristic prelude : —

"All the world knew Lord Eldon to be a great lawyer, but no one was aware, until Mr. Horace Twiss published the fact, that the great ex-Chancellor was a poet of no mean pretensions. His Lordship's lyrics to his Bessie contain all the sweetness of Spencer, combined with the copiousness of Coke, all the melody of Moore, with nearly all the precision of Petersdorff. We are happy in being able to furnish a specimen."

41. Law at our Boarding House. By A. C. Gordon. *Scribner's Monthly*, May, 1880, p. 100.

43. The Lawyer's Valentine. By John G. Saxe, St. Albans, Vermont, Aug., 1844. *Knickerbocker Magazine*, Vol. XXIX., p. 266.

45. The Lawyer's Suit. By John G. Saxe.

47. To —— the Lawyer. *Punch*, Vol. II. (1842), p. 66.

50. A Moan from the San Francisco Bar. Miss Mary McH—, a young lady remarkable for her studious habits and varied accomplishments (daughter of a much respected Louisiana judge, now deceased), was a short time since graduated in the academic department and at the law school of the University of California, and admitted to practice under circumstances which seemed to be auspicious for a forensic success on her part, if such success were at all possible for a lady of remarkably gentle and retiring disposition. It is now, however, announced that she is about to marry the genial landscape painter K——, a jolly good fellow, famous for his brilliant renditions upon canvas of California scenery, and for his charming ability in singing Scotch melodies.

Miss Mary's modesty and beauty, and the present editor's gallantry, make the following quotation imperative : —

> Novella, a young Bolognese,
>> The daughter of a learned law-doctor.
> Who had with all the subtleties
>> Of old and modern jurists stock'd her,
> Was so exceeding fair, 'tis said,
>> And over hearts held such dominion,
> That when her father, sick in bed,
> Or busy, sent her in his stead
>> To lecture on the Code Justinian,

> She had a curtain drawn before her,
> Lest if her charms were seen, the students
> Should let their young eyes wander o'er her,
> And quite forget their jurisprudence.
> —*Notes and Queries*, Vol. III., 2nd Series, p. 120.

52. A Professional Love Song. *Punch*, Vol. XLVII. (1864) p. 51.

55. The Lawyer's Stratagem. Originally appearing in the *Boston Post*, the hot-bed of so much American wit and humor; republished in *Harper's Monthly*, Vol. XV., p. 566 (Sept. 1857), and there ascribed to Brown.

57. Love and Law. A legend of Boston. By John G. Saxe, from "The Masquerade and Other Poems," p. 75.

62. In Woman's Praise. By Hon. Sheppard Barclay, St. Louis. *The Forum*, Vol. I., p. 189.

65. An Old Saw. *Harper's Monthly*. Vol. XIII. (1856), p. 724.

66. Law. A comic song, air, "Malbrook." Reprinted in *Albany Law Journal*, Vol. I.

Good songs, as well as great works in other fields of literature, may be traced back to obscure and lowly sources and still remain anonymous. Of this 'Malbrook" (Malbrongh) is a striking illustration. When the Arabs overran Gothic Spain an air was born harmonious with clash of cymbals, and the roll and beat of the drum. Chateaubriand heard it sung by the Arabs in the moslem camps in Palestie, and asserts that it had been carried there by the Crusaders, and that Godfrey de Bouillon, who with his Christian Cavaliers had pitched their tents about Jerusalem, returned to Europe with a sauntering march, humming the air, and beating the time as the gods might do in an opera overture.

It remained endemic in western Europe breaking out spamodically now and then until the days of Malborough, when the Gauls, among other bits of gibing at their great enemy, started a song to the old air; the "mironton" of the refrain being accompanied with a beating to represent the drum, and the higher strain, the rolling of the drum. Malbrook died, was buried for generations, and until Madame Poitrine sang it as a lullaby for the infant dauphin in 1781. Marie Antoinette, charmed by her baby's cradle song, sang it herself. It was caught by her courtiers, and the beribboned descendants of the crusaders revived the air which had once floated over the cymbal-clashing, mail-clad ports of Saladin in the Holy Land. It soon spread though Versailles, Paris, and throughout France. The Malbrough of the song was a crusader who died in battle, and whose lady climbed the tower looking out for her lord, as did the mother of Sisera, who looked out at a window and cried through the latice, "Why is his chariot so long in coming? Why tarry the wheels of his chariots? Have they not sped? Have they not divided the spoil?"

Malbrook's funeral procession became the popular subject of decorative art. It was deliniated in caricature, and painted on fans with a little tower and an immense lady at the top.

M. Las Cases states that Napoleon never mounted his charger for battle without humming this air, and that he heard him hum it but a little time before his death. Beaumarchais, in 1784, introduced the song in his drama, "The Marriage of Figaro," in the song of "The Pretty Page with Dimpled Chin." The warlike air is here made to tell a story of loving languor:

> Là, près d'une fontaine
> (Que mon cœur, mon cœur a de peine).

A different air and libretto was unfortunately inserted in the opera, but Beethoven, in 1813, honored it with a place in his "Battle Symphonie." Englishmen retaliated burlesquing the song, and the bluff army successors of Malbrook and their recruiting officers sang it thus:

> We like to take our ease, sir,
> With a damsel on our knees, sir,
> And give her a hearty squeeze, sir,
> To drive dull care away.

Thence it extended its conquest to the Student's Cloister, and uttered the confessions:

> We think it is no sin, sir,
> To take the Freshman in, sir,
> And rob them of their tin, sir,
> To drive dull care away.

It has invaded the innocence of the school room, and we think the rakish air has done duty as a revival hymn. At the present day the air will be more promptly recognized with the convivial words, "We won't go Home till Morning." So this nameless or many-named vagrant has come down anonymous still. But as to the theory of its origin see Grove's Dictionary of Music and Musicians, Vol. II., p. 290.

69. The Annuity. By George Outram. George Outram, the author, was born at Glasgow, March 25, 1805, and died there in 1856. He was called to the Scottish bar in 1827, but devoted some attention to journalism, being part proprietor of the *Glasgow Herald.* He wrote a number of humorous and satirical pieces, and a collection of his verses, entitled "Legal Lyrics," was published after his death by Blackwood & Sons. *Wilson's Poets and Poetry of Scotland,* Vol. II., p. 533.

The following note is from the "Centenary" of *The Glasgow Herald,* by J. H. Stoddart, Esq., editor of the *Herald.*

"Mr. George Outram, advocate, was appointed editor (*Glasgow Herald*) on Mr. Hunter's resignation (May, 1837), and at the same time he was admitted a partner. Unlike his predecessor, he was of a singularly retiring disposition, and took no personal part in the public affairs or social gatherings of the city. He was, however, a man of fine genius, and his heart was as good as his head. By those who knew him well he was warmly beloved, and no man deserved better to be beloved. His poetical writings are now known to a large circle, although the author never would consent to their publication. His songs are rich in illustration, and contain the very essence of fun. Latterly Mr. Outram's health became infirm, and he retired from the active discharge of his editorial duties a few years before his death, which took place at his residence, Rosmore, on the Holy Loch, on the 16th September, 1856. He was interred in Warriston Cemetery, Edinburgh. Mr. Outram's family still holds his interest in the *Herald* property. On Mr. Outram's retirement I was appointed to take his place."

76. The Annuitant's Answer. *Wilson's Poets and Poetry of Scotland,* Vol. II., p. 534. At a dinner given by Dr. Robert Chambers, in Edinburgh, to Outram and a select party of friends, these verses were sung in character by Mrs. R. C. after "The Annuity" had been sung by Peter Frazer. The "honest Maurice" mentioned in the last stanza is the late Maurice Lothian of Edinburgh.

79. A Fragment. By George Outram.

80. Minimum de Malis. *Harper's Monthly,* Vol. L., p. 928. Concerning going to law on a small matter, the following from the latin of George Buchanan may be regarded as sound.

81. Lay of Gascoigne Justice. A parody on Macaulay's "Lays of Ancient Rome." By John William Smith. *Law Magazine,* Vol. XXXV., p. 189; see also 12 *Notes and Queries* (1855), p. 406. For a delightful sketch of the life of this eminent jurist, by Samuel Warren, see *Blackwood,* Vol. LXI., pp. 129-161.

87. **Ye Juvenile Offender by a Puzzled Magistrate.** By T. Bruce Johnston. *Advocate,* Edinburgh. *Journal of Jurisprudence,* Vol. XXV., p. 107.

89. **The Law of Marriage** By George Outram. See note to page 69.

92. **The Tourists' Matrimonial Guide Through Scotland.** By Lord Neaves. Published in "Songs and Verses, Social and Scientific."

96. **The Purchasing of Land.**

98. **The Jolly Testator Who Makes His Own Will.** By a contributor to *Blackwood* (Lord Neaves). Copied in *American Law Review,* Vol. VII., p. 387; see also "Songs and Verses, Social and Scientific."

Any verse, whether permitted by gods, men, or booksellers, or no, written by a man who is entitled to the following biography at the hands of his associates, is deserving of attention, even without the wit which prevades it:—

LORD NEAVES.

" There was a boy, a bright-eyed boy, the dux of all the school,
Who kept the place at Midsummer which he had won at Yule;
Thro' Horace, Terence, Juvenal, he cantered at his case,
Nor boggled at the hardest bits of old Thucydides.
No mathematics daunted him; he needed small instruction,
To dive at once into the depths of algebra and fluxion.
There's not a dry eye in the school the day on which he leaves,
Yet little did the rector know that boy would be Lord Neaves.

" There was a lad, an eager lad, who studied day and night,
Whose spirit through all realms of thought pursued a lofty flight,
Who walked away with every prize in every class at college
And left unopened not one gate of all the gates of knowledge,
And yet he was no cold recluse but debonnair and free,
As one who feels that social ties exalt philosophy.
Professors smiling shake his hand; the principal believes,
The day may come when that fine lad may live to be Lord Neaves.

" There was a man, an earnest man, who took to study law,
He waded through old Morrison, he swam ahead of Shaw.
He took the marrow out of Stair, the entrails out of Bell;
He sucked the egg of Erskine, and left nothing but the shell.

He quoted case and precedent, unravelled every twist,
From darkened legal quiddity he cleared away the mist.
The judges gaze in wonderment and whisper in their sleeves,
Both Whigs and Tories will agree to make that man Lord Neaves.

"There was a father who had wed a fair and gentle dame,
And more than all his honors prized a husband's, father's name.
Who as he trod the round of life thro' all it's weary miles,
Found ever at his own fireside sweet faces and fair smiles.
Ah ! better than ambition's fire, or triumph, or success,
Soft eyes that look into our own, loved hands our own that press:
'Tis never for himself alone a father toils, achieves,
'Tis for the well-known voice that says, 'Papa will be Lord Neaves.'

"There is a judge whom all the land esteems as wise and good,
Most fixed in what he deems the right, yet never harsh nor rude ;
Clear in his office, faithful, just, more pleased to bless than ban,
And proving that the soundest law comes from the kindliest man.
In him the dux of all the school and student ripe survives ;—
Youth's freshness, age's wisdom, still unite the noblest lives,
And every compeer lovingly and with delight receives
The valued friend, the honored judge, the unspoilt man, Lord
      Neaves."

101. Will of William Ruffell, Esq., of Shimpling, Suffolk.
From *Notes and Queries*. 1st Series, Vol. XII., p. 81.

104. A Lawyer's Will. *Legal Observer*, Vol. X. (1835), p. 16.
This quaint and characteristic production was written by Mr. John
Cooper Grocott, an octogenarian Liverpool solicitor, recently
deceased. Mr. Grocott was the author of "An Index of Familiar
Quotation, Ancient and Modern," a work which has passed through
several editions. *Notes and Queries*, 5th Series, Vol. II. (1874),
p. 226.

106. Will of Joshua West, of the Six Clerk's Office, Chancery
Lane. Dated December 13, 1804. *Notes and Queries*, Vol. XII.,
p. 82.

107. Will of James Bigsby, of Manningtree. Dated February
4, 1839. *Notes and Queries*, 1st Series, Vol. XII., p. 86.

110. Wills Without Lawyers. *Punch*, Vol. XVI. (1849), p. 2.

111. Make Thy Will. *Punch*, Vol. LVI. (1869), p. 127.

113. A Question of Testamentary Disposition. The subject of these verses is alluded to in a letter from Sir William Blackstone, addressed to Mr. Richmond, at Sparsholt, near Wantage, Berks, Arundel Street, January 28, 1775:—

"I have trespassed so far on y^r patience that I am almost afraid to venture any farther. But I happen'd t'other day upon a case in a civil law book, wch I should be glad to know how you imagine chancery w^d decide. A man dies and leaves his wife with child, and by his will ordains that, if his wife brought forth a son, ye son sh^d have 2 3ds and ye mother one 3d of the estate; if a daughter, then ye wife to have 2 and ye daughter 1 3d. The wife brought twins, a boy and girl. Qu. How shall ye estate be divided? N. B. We must suppose a jointure, or something in bar of dower." 1 *Legal Observer*, 12.

115. Canons of Descent. *Law Reporter*, Vol. I., p. 184. From a London magazine. Versified from Blackstone's Commentaries, by an apprentice of the law.

117. Rules of Descent in the United States, as Laid Down in Kent's Commentaries. By T. W. Davidson of Lexington, Virginia, in *Southern Law Journal.* Copied in *Albany Law Journal*, Vol. XXIII., p. 140.

120. Variation of the Rule in Shelly's Case. *Washington Law Reporter*, Vol. IX., p. 221.

123. St. Peter vs. The Lawyer. Printed on a sheet of foolscap. At the head is a cut representing St. Peter opening the gates of Heaven to a lawyer desirous of entering, but whom the Apostle on recognizing his profession refuses to admit. There is no date or author's name attached. *Notes and Queries*, Vol. XII. (1855). p. 44.

127. Justice and the Lawyer. From Edward Moore's "Fables for the Female Sex," London, 1744, 1849.

130. The Devil and the Lawyer. Reprinted in *Western Jurist*, Vol. XV., p. 287.

Perhaps we should not have omitted in this connection the lines of John G. Saxe from the "Money King and Other Poems."

HOW THE LAWYERS GOT A PATRON SAINT.

A LEGEND OF BRETAGNE.

A lawyer of Brittany, once on a time,
  When business was flagging at home,
Was sent as a legate to Italy's clime,
  To confer with the Father at Rome.

And what was the message the minister brought?
  To the Pope he preferred a complaint
That each other profession a Patron had got,
  While the Lawyers had never a Saint!

"Very true," said his holiness,—smiling to find
  An attorney so civil and pleasant,—
"But my very last Saint is already assigned,
  And I can't make a new one at present.

"To choose from the *Bar* it were fittest, I think;
  Perhaps you've a man in your eye"—
And his Holiness here gave a mischievous wink
  To a Cardinal sitting near by.

But the lawyer replied, in a lawyer like way,
  "I know what is modest, I hope;
I didn't come hither, allow me to say,
  To proffer advice to the Pope!"

"Very well," said his Holiness, "then we will do
  The best that may fairly be done;
It don't seem exactly the thing, it is true,
  That the Law should be Saint-less alone.

"To treat your profession as well as I can,
  And leave you no cause of complaint,
I propose, as the only quite feasible plan,
  To give you a second-hand Saint.

"To the neighboring church you will presently go,
  And this is the plan I advise:—
First, say a few *aves*—a hundred or so—
  Then carefully bandage your eyes;

"Then (saying more *aves*) go groping around,
  And, touching one object alone,
The Saint you are seeking will quickly be found,
  For the first that you touch is your own."

The lawyer did as his Holiness said,
  Without an omission or flaw;
Then, taking the bandages off from his head,
  What do you think he saw?

There was St. Michael (figured in paint)
   Subduing the Father of Evil ;
And the lawyer, exclaiming " Be *thou* our Saint !"
   Was touching the form of the DEVIL !

For the legend of St. Evona, a lawyer of Brittanic. See *Notes and Queries*, 1st Series, Vol. I., p. 152.

132. The Farmer and the Counsellor. Nimmo's Humorous Poetry, p. 230.

134. The Counsel's Tear. *Punch*, Vol. XXI. (1851), p. 239.

136. Baines Carew Gentleman. *Babb Ballads.* By Wm. S. Gilbert.

140. Poor Richards' Opinion. By Dr. Franklin (1798), *Harper's Monthly*, Vol. XII. (1856), p. 139.

141. The Rush to the Bar. By Alex. Nicolson, now sheriff substitute of Kirkcudbright, Scotland, a famous Gaelic scholar. The above poem, originally appearing in *Journal of Jurisprudence*, Vol. XV., p. 881, Dec. 23, 1870, is taken from " Ballads of the Bench and Bar or Idle Lays of Parliament House," privately printed, 1882, at the Edinburgh University Press, by T. and A. Constable.

144. The Song of the Intrant. From *Journal of Jurisprudence.* Vol. XIX., p. 459, also republished in " Ballads of the Bench and Bar."

148. Crossing the Rubicon. From *Journal of Jurisprudence*, Vol. XIX., p. 242, also republished in " Ballads of the Bench and Bar."

151. Advice to a Young Lawyer. By Justice Joseph Story, *Law Reporter*, Vol. VIII., p. 252. *Life*, Vol. II., p. 620.

154. On Hearing an Argument in Court. By Justice Joseph Story. *Life*, Vol. II., p. 413.

155. The Briefless Barrister. By John G. Saxe. Revised after first publication in *The Knickerbocker*, and republished in his poems.

158. Elegy Written in the Temple Gardens. First appeared in the *Legal Examiner*, afterwards in *American Jurist*, Vol. XVI., p. 244 (Oct. 1836), credited to former serial.

165. The Brief. *Punch*, Vol. X. (1846), p. 148. Sung in one of *Punch's* legal " At Homes."

166. The First Client. *Scribner's Monthly*, Vol. XIV. (1877), p. 575. [A legal ditty to be sung without chorus to the air of "The King's Old Courtier."] By Irwin Russell, who died in New Orleans, December 23, 1879. See memorial lines by H. C. Bunner in *Puck*. Also in *Scribner*, Vol. XIX., p. 799.

170. Monodie on the Death of an Only Client. Attributed to *Punch*. *Albany Law Journal*, Vol. I., p. 369.

173. A Successful Career. *Journal of Jurisprudence*, Vol. XVIII., p. 477. Republished in "Ballads of the Bench and Bar."

174. The Vision and the Reality. By "a Lady" and Joel Parker. *American Law Review*, Vol. X., p. 265.

177. A Whimsical Attorney's Bill. Published in *Harper's Monthly*, Vol. XLIV., p. 476, as copied from an English grammar of 1799, and entitled : —

> "A bill of charges justly due
> From A. B. C. to S. T. U."

179. The Bachelor's Dream. By John Rankine, Advocate, Edinburgh. Republished in "Ballads of the Bench and Bar," from *Journal of Jurisprudence*, Vol. XXII., p. 155. "The following verses were found in the editor's box at the Parliament House. They seem to be the result of a nocturnal visitation which had disturbed the repose of some contributor to the Advocate's Widows' Fund, who had imprudently retired to rest after endeavoring to master the contents of the Actuarie's Report some time previous to the meeting of the 20th ult."

182. My Widow. By David Crichton, author of the "Circuiteer's Lament," see p. 221, *post*. *Journal of Jurisprudence*, Vol. XXIV., p. 51. By an involuntary contributor to what he thinks the most iniquitous institution of the nineteenth century — "The Advocate's Widows' Fund."

185. Monboddo. From "Songs and Verses, Social and Scientific," (Lord Neaves), also in *Journal of Jurisprudence*, Vol. XII., p. 280. To justify the insertion of these verses among the Lyrics of the Law, we may quote the *Journal of Jurisprudence :*

"It would be out of place here, except that Scotch lawyers have certainly a class feeling which will be well satisfied, that one of his successors should so gallantly vindicate the right of Lord Monboddo to be considered the true author of what is unfairly called the 'Darwinian' doctrine of the origin of species. Every Scotch lawyer is bound to dispute Mr. Darwin's title to the invention of this theory."

186. The Process of Wakening. By George Outram. A proceeding which might be deemed analogous to a bill of revivor in American Chancery Proceedings.

189. Soumin and Roumin. By George Outram.

192. The Rule to Compute. *Punch*, Vol. I. (1841), p. 273. "Ballads of the Briefless."

193. Signing a Plea. *Punch*, Vol. I. (1841), p. 273. "Ballads of the Briefless."

194. A Misjoinder. *Harper's Monthly*, Vol. XVI., p. 570.

196. The Orderly Parts of Pleading. *Legal Gazette*, Vol. IV., p. 59. "The orderly parts of pleading at common law, together with the rules which tend to the production of an issue. A metrical composition by Dr. S. D. Sibbet."

Just here we offer as an encore, to the air of "Co-ca-che-lunk," Mr. Irving Browne's "Psalm of Law." See Browne's "Humorous Phases of the Law," revised edition, p. 240.

A PSALM OF LAW.

What the heart of the Codifier said to the Pleader.

Tell me not, in accents croaking,
"Brevity's an empty dream";
What's the use, with verbal cloaking,
To make things other than they seem?

Law is real; and law's expensive;
Special pleading's not its goal;
Rhetoric and tape make pensive
Many a weary client's soul.

To orate, or rouse to passion
In your pleading's not the way;
State your case in simple fashion,
Let the judge see what's to pay.

Law is long and time is fleeting,
And our lips, dull habit's slave,
Are, forgetting fact, repeating
The old forms our fathers gave.

In the field of litigation,
   In the strife of good and evil,
With straightforward allegation
   Tell the truth and shame the devil.

Trust not Humphrey, Barbour, Chitty;
   Let dead cases bury their dead;
With stale lies 'tis surely pity
   To bother any judge's head!

Lives of pleaders all remind us,
   We may make our lives a bore,
And, departing, leave behind us
   Pleas choke full of useless lore;—

Precedents that perhaps another,
   Doomed by cruel fate to find,—
Some perplexed and anxious brother,
   Reading, shall quite lose his mind!

Sell your form books for waste paper;
   State the facts at any rate;
Hesitating how to shape a
   Pleading—why, abbreviate.

199. Jury Trial in Days of Edward I. Attributed to John Gibson Lockhart. This translation in volume ten of the *Journal of Jurisprudence*, p. 51, is preceded by the following note: "It may amuse our readers to compare with our modern feelings the earliest strictures on that 'palladium of our liberties' with which we happen to be acquainted. These are contained in an Anglo-Norman ballad of the reign of Edward I., the author of which seems to have had excellent opportunities of judging of the capacity of the jurymen of his day. It seems to us to be a singularly striking and picturesque expression of individual feeling, and probably of popular feeling also. We extract a translation from the 'Janus,' a long-forgotten Edinburgh miscellany in which the writers are anonymous. But it is known that Wilson and Lockhart were the principal contributors, and it is impossible not to recognize in the ease and fluency the simplicity and vigor of the lines, the accomplished hand of the translator of the Spanish ballads."

202. The Pet of the British Jury. *Punch*, Vol. XXXI. (1856), p. 23.

205. Digest of Lord ——'s Evidence before the Royal Commission as to Jury Trial. *Journal of Jurisprudence*, Vol. XIV., p. 623, signed G. J.

206. Light from an Eminent S. S. C. *Journal of Jurisprudence*, Vol. XV., p. 642.

208. The Jury Law Victim. Dedicated to the Attorney-General. *Punch*, Vol. LXII. (1872), p. 211.

210. Juror No. 6. *Legal Gazette*, Vol. III., p. 29.

212 The Home Circuit. Songs of the Circuit; The Home. *Punch*, Vol. VI. (1844), p. 136.

213. The Mississippi Witness. By Irwin Russell. *Scribner*, Vol. XIII (1876), p. 236. See note to 166, "The First Client."

216. The Demise of Doe and Roe. *Punch*, Vol. XXIII. (1852), p. 53.

221. The Circuiteer's Lament. By David Crichton, Advocate, Edinburgh. *Journal of Jurisprudence*, Vol. XVI., p. 377. Reprinted in "Ballads of the Bench and Bar," with title of "The Ex-Circuiteer's Lament."

225. A Case of Libel. Thomas Moore. Collected Works, (Little, Brown & Co. 1856), Vol. III., p. 78.

228. Report of an Adjudged Case. William Cowper. Poetical Works (Little, Brown & Co. 1853), Vol. I., p. 210.

230. Hat vs. Wig. Thomas Moore. Collected Works (Little, Brown & Co. 1856), Vol. III., p. 68. At the midnight funeral of the Duke of York, in St. George's Chapel, Windsor, in January, 1827, the night was bitterly severe. No carpet nor matting had been laid on the bare stones. Lord Eldon placed his cocked hat under his feet and stood upon it. Stapleton says that Canning suggested to him the act that probably saved the old man's life. Unhappily Canning had not taken the same care of his own, his death resulting from a cold caught on that occasion. Hall's "Retrospect of a Long Life," p. 91.

234. The Case Altered. Humorous Poetry, Nimmo, p. 260.

237. A Settlement Case. Reported in Burrow's Settlement Cases, p. 367.

239. Punch in Chancery. *Punch*, Vol. V. (1843), p. 54.

241. State vs. Day; The Law of Husband and Wife. By Judge R. M. Charlton of Savannah, Georgia, Reporter of Georgia Decisions from 1811-1837. Published in the *American Jurist*, Vol. XX. (1838), p. 237. Collections of his poems were published, Boston, 1833, New York, 1843, died 1854.

248. Cooper vs. Bloodgood, a "riprarian" poem; or, **License and Lease.** By William Paterson. *New Jersey Law Journal*, Vol. IV., p. 127.

253. Craft vs Boite. By R. H. Thornton. *Washington Law Reporter*, Vol. VI., p. 92. The case is reported in 1 Saunders, p. 242.

257. Regina vs. Gallars. *Punch's* version of the case of Regina *v.* Gallears is a clear statement of the case officially reported in 1 Denison's Crown Cases, p. 501, and also in 2 Carrington & Kirwin, 981; the case cited therein, Regina *v.* Cox, will be found in 1 Carrington & Kirwin, 494, the decision being that "An indictment for stealing 'three eggs of the value of twopence of the goods and chattels of S. H.' is bad, for not stating the species of eggs, because it does not show that the eggs stolen might not be such as are not the subject of larceny."

259. Lewis vs. State. 19 Kansas, p. 266. In the nineteenth volume of Reports of the Supreme Court of Kansas, this versification is given with the following:—

"*Reporter's Note.* The peculiar features of the foregoing case of The State *v.* Lewis seem to justify the inserting here of the 'poetical report' thereof, written by Eugene F. Ware, Esq., attorney at law of Fort Scott, and which he published in the *Fort Scott Daily Monitor* of the 10th March, 1878.

261. Kuhn et al vs. Jewett, Receiver. 32 N. J. Eq. 647. By William B. Gourley, in *New Jersey Law Journal*, Vol. III., p. 223.

266. Cushing vs. Blake. 29 N. J. Eq. 399; 30 N. J. Eq. 689. By William B. Gourley. *New Jersey Law Journal*, Vol. IV., p. 96.

268. Commonwealth vs. McAfee. 108 Mass. 458. By C. P. Greenough. *American Law Review*, Vol. XI. (1877), p. 332.

269. Opinion of the Justices. 106 Mass. p. 604. By C. P. Greenough. *American Law Review*, Vol. XI (1877), p. 333.

270. Luther vs. Worcester. 97 Mass. p. 272. By C. P. Greenough. *American Law Review*, Vol. XI. (1877), p. 333.

271. The Lad Frae Cockpen. *Journal of Jurisprudence*, Vol. XXXII., p. 39. A married man, who was butler to a gentleman in the parish of Cockpen, went to Ireland, where he obtained a similar situation both as a butler and a married man. He was tried for bigamy before Baron Deasy and a jury at Maryborough Assizes, the learned judge remarking that they had often heard of the Laird of Cockpen, but now they had his butler. The prisoner was convicted and sentenced to five years penal servitude.

"The Laird of Cockpen," a Scotch ballad, is said to have been written by Lady Nairn, and refers to the lands of Cockpen situated about seven miles from Edinburgh. While Charles II. was in Scotland suffering the censure of austere presbyterianism, his chief confident and associate was the Laird of Cockpen, called by the nicknaming manners of those times "Blythe Cockpen." Cockpen followed Charles to the Hague, and by his skill in playing Scottish tunes, and his sagacity and wit, delighted the merry monarch, and played to him his favorite tune, "Brose and Butter," when he went to bed and before he awakened. At the Restoration (1660) Cockpen was forgotten, and he wandered upon the lands he once had owned poor and unfriended. His letters to the court were not presented or regarded, and he resorted to his wits to gain the ear of the king. Ingratiating himself with the king's organist, he was requested by him to play the organ before the king at divine service. Cockpen played with exquisite skill, yet never attracted his majesty's eye. But at the close of the service, instead of playing the tune in common use, he played up 'Brose and Butter." The organist was at once summoned into the presence of the king. "My Liege, it was not me," he cried, and dropped upon his knees. "You," cried his majesty, in a delirium of rapture, "you could never play it in your life. Where is the man? Let me see him." Cockpen presented himself on his knees. "Ah, Cockpen, is that you? Lord, man, I was like to dance coming out of the church." " I once danced, too," said Cockpen, " but that was when I had land of my own to dance on." "Come with me," said the king, taking him by the hand, "you shall dance to ' Brose and Butter' on your own lands again to the nineteenth generation "; and he was as good as his word. 8 *Notes and Queries*, 2d Series, 123.

273. Owen Kerr vs. Owen Kerr. *Western Jurist*, Vol. V. p. 138.

274. Tuff vs. Warman. 5 C. B. N. S. p. 573. *Law Magazine and Review*, Vol. XVII., p. 234.

280. Hopkins vs. W. P. R. R. Co. By an officious Reporter. 50 California Reports, p. 190. Action for damages for creating and maintaining a nuisance. S. W. Sanderson, for appellant. The acts complained of are *damnum absque injuria.* Budd, McKinne, and Martin, for respondent. Appellant had no right to construct road in front of respondent's residence, and if it had, the road should have been so constructed as not to form an obstruction or nuisance. . . . .

Per Curiam, McKinstry, J.:

"The court below also erred in admitting evidence of the purpose for which the portion of the street beneath the shadow of the defendant's culvert was used. The *employees* of defendant were not *moving within the scope of their employment in the acts complained of,* but on their own account; and it does not appear that the *additional easement was enjoyed* exclusively by the defendant. The doctrine *respondeat superior* does not apply."

We are told that the unfortunate plaintiff and respondent in disgust sold his pleasant residence, and emigrated to Alabama or Georgia, or to some region still intractable to the miracles of railway engineering.

290. McVey vs. Hennigan. "Ballads of the Bench and Bar."

LEGAL RECREATIONS,

COMBINING

ROMANCE, POETRY, WIT, HUMOR, AND LAW.

Good Law and Good Reading.

Eight Volumes now ready as follows:

Browne's Humorous Phases of the Law, 16 mo. Cloth,		\$1.50
Browne's Common Words and Phrases,	"	1.50
Proffatt's Curiosities and Law of Wills,	"	1.50
Paget's Judicial Puzzles,	"	1.50
Rogers' Law of the Road,	"	1.50
Rogers' Law of the House,	"	1.50
Baldwin's Flush Times in Alabama,	"	1.50
Croke's Lyrics of the Law,	"	1.50

IN PRESS.

POEMS OF THE LAW,

EDITED BY

J. GREENBAG CROKE,

EMBRACING

GENERAL AVERAGE, - - -	*Wm. Allen Butler*
YE BALLADE OF CHANCERY, - -	*From Punch*
JACOB HOMNIUM'S HOSS, - - -	*Wm. M. Thackeray*
THE ROMAN LAWYER IN JERUSALEM, -	*W. W. Story*
THE CONVEYANCER'S GUIDE, - - -	
THE PLEADER'S GUIDE, - - -	*J. Anstey*

www.ingramcontent.com/pod-product-compliance
Lightning Source LLC
Chambersburg PA
CBHW060549030726
47498CB00005B/1327